With shaking hands, Maddie put the paper back on the desk. She felt as though she had stepped into a dark, twisted place where everything was upside down and nothing was what it seemed. Clive appeared so nice . . . so *normal!* They even liked the same kind of music.

But these weren't the writings of a normal person.

The Lancaster Witch

by Carol H. Behrman

cover illustration by Bill Dodge

*To Edward, and to our friends in Morecambe,
Kathleen and Harold*

Published by Willowisp Press
801 94th Avenue North, St Petersburg, Florida 33702

Copyright © 1993 by Willowisp Press,
a division of PAGES, Inc.

Printed in the United States of America

2 4 6 8 10 9 7 5 3

ISBN 0-87406-645-X

One

"*C*LIVE?" Maddie Stoner almost choked on a mouthful of mashed potatoes. "Since when do I have a cousin named Clive, and why is he coming here now?" she asked, beginning to cough.

"Drink some water," her mother said.

Maddie managed to swallow the potatoes. "So?" she insisted. "Who *is* he, and when did he get to be my cousin?" She looked from her mother to her father, waiting for someone to clear up the mystery.

"Clive's always been your cousin," said Mrs. Stoner. "He's almost a year older than you—going on fourteen."

"How come I've never heard of him before?"

"Actually, Clive is not *exactly* your cousin," her father explained. "He's more like a second cousin. Or..." Mr. Stoner paused, and scratched his chin thoughtfully. "Maybe describing him as a third cousin would be more accurate." He nodded. "Yes, a third cousin—that's it."

Maddie was far from satisfied. She stared at her mother, hoping for an explanation. It drove Maddie wild the way her parents sometimes talked all around a subject before coming to the point. "Well, Mom?"

"Eat your meal before it gets cold, Maddie," said her mother.

Maddie groaned and jabbed a piece of chicken with her fork. "*Well?*"

"It's very simple," Mrs. Stoner said. "Clive is the son of my cousin, Deborah. Deborah's family moved to England a long time ago. Then Deborah married an Englishman, and we lost touch with each other, except for Christmas cards and an occasional letter."

Maddie remembered holiday mail with an airmail stamp and a foreign postmark.

"Anyway," her mother continued, "Deborah telephoned last night and asked if Clive could visit."

Maddie wondered whether it was her imagination, or whether her mother was trying to avoid looking at her. "Okay, so we have cousins in England. But why is this Clive kid suddenly coming here?"

Mrs. Stoner stood up. "Please clear the table, Maddie. I'll bring out dessert."

Maddie picked up the dinner plates and began to load them in the dishwasher. "You didn't answer my question, Mom. Why is he coming?"

"Do you want lemon Jell-O or a donut?"

"Both!" Maddie always felt annoyed when adults ignored her questions.

While Maddie helped her mother bring out the dessert, Mr. Stoner, who never ate sweets, stood up and pushed in his chair. "I'm going out to mow the lawn before it gets too dark," he said.

Maddie sat down again. "Come on, Mom. Are you going to tell me about this Clive or not?" She poked at her dark hair, trying to push a stubborn curl back into place.

Mrs. Stoner shrugged. "There's not much to tell. Clive wants to visit the United States, and Deborah asked if he could stay with us."

"And you said yes?"

"Of course. He's family." Mrs. Stoner's tone was final.

Maddie nibbled at her donut. She sensed that there was more to this unexpected visit than a sudden telephone call from England. But there was no way of prying more information out of her mom now. Meanwhile, she had to share this news with her best friend.

"Can I call Chloe?" she asked.

Her mother nodded. Maddie dashed to her room and dialed Chloe's number. She listened impatiently to the ringing at the other end.

"Hello?" Chloe answered on the fourth ring.

"Chloe! You'll never guess!"

"I'll bet I can."

"No!" Maddie was sure of this. "Never in a million years."

"Let's see... hmm..."

Maddie knew that Chloe must be biting her lip.

"I know!" said Chloe. "Luke Kramer asked you out."

Maddie couldn't help laughing. "I wish he

really had!" she said.

Luke Kramer was the best-looking and most popular guy in seventh grade. Maddie figured the chance of being asked out by him was zero with a capital Z. Not that she had ever been on a date with anyone else either. Sometimes she and Tommy Willis went out for ice cream. But those weren't *dates*. Those were just going for ice cream with the boy across the street, exactly as they had been doing since third grade. No big deal.

"No," Maddie said, "it's something even better."

Chloe tired of the game quickly. "So, what's up?"

"Would you believe that I have a mysterious cousin named Clive, and he's coming to stay with us for two weeks?"

"Clive!" Chloe giggled. "Get real! What kind of name is Clive?"

"He's English," Maddie told her. "He's coming on Saturday, and"— she lowered her voice to a whisper even though she was alone—"there's something weird about the whole thing."

"What?"

"I don't know," Maddie said. "My mom keeps dodging the issue. It must be pretty bad." Maddie glanced at her bookshelves while she waited for Chloe's reply. They were a mess. She wondered if she should straighten up her whole room before their guest arrived.

"Maybe this Clive is a teddy boy," Chloe suggested.

"A *what?*"

Chloe hesitated. "I don't really know," she admitted. "But I remember seeing some kind of reference to 'teddy boy' in a book about teen gangs in England."

"You mean, he might be a criminal?" *Maybe Clive's parents are sending him here to keep him out of jail,* Maddie thought suddenly. That would explain why her mom was being so cagey.

"How old is this guy?" Chloe asked.

"Almost fourteen."

"Then he can't be a teddy," Chloe said confidently. "I'm pretty sure they're older." She paused. "Did you say he's practically fourteen? Gee, I wonder if he's cute."

"That's all you can think about!" Maddie said with a chuckle. "What I wonder is what's so strange about him that my mom doesn't want to tell me?"

"I've got it!" Chloe announced. "You know all those really neat English rock groups? Maybe he's into music his parents think is really strange. They could be trying to get him away from it."

"So you think he's some kind of rocker?" Maddie asked, giving the idea some thought.

"Maybe," said Chloe, "and hey! they're all so *cute*. Maddie, you are *so* lucky!"

Chloe's excitement was contagious. Maddie had been dreading having to drag some nerd from England around with her—especially if he was some kind of tough guy in trouble with the law. But maybe having him around *wouldn't* be so bad. Maybe it would be good—even great. As Maddie pictured what it would be like to have another kid living in their house—a boy, at that!—she could almost cast doubt from her mind altogether.

But not quite.

*   *   *   *   *

Clive was scheduled to arrive a week later

on Saturday morning. Maddie and her parents drove to Kennedy Airport in New York from their home in suburban Fairmount, New Jersey. It was a brilliant, sunny day. White clouds dotted the sky.

As she waited at the airport's arrivals area, Maddie thought longingly of the Fairmount community pool. School had let out for the summer earlier in the week, and all the kids would be there. Spending time with them at the pool was a lot more tempting than being with her parents at the airport. Besides, she was eager to try out her new white swimsuit.

But Maddie's curiosity about her cousin won out. He was like a puzzle with missing pieces.

So here she was at the airport, staring at a big board that displayed information about incoming and outgoing flights. It showed that the plane from London had already landed. Passengers were beginning to come through the gate. Maddie watched as they filed past her.

Men and women in business suits carried attaché cases. A stocky, balding man in a gray raincoat impatiently shoved past slower-moving travelers. A young woman holding a baby and accompanied by a bearded man gave Maddie a brief smile. Maddie smiled back distractedly as her eyes darted toward a lanky teenage boy a few feet behind them.

She gasped. Right behind him was a tall woman wearing a long black dress. She had dark hair pulled into a severe bun over a thin neck. But it was the woman's face that made Maddie catch her breath. Long and angular with high cheekbones, the face was the palest Maddie had ever seen—so pale it was almost white. The woman's hand rested lightly on the boy's shoulder.

"That must be him!" Mrs. Stoner announced. "Clive!" she called. "Clive!"

At that moment, a man hurrying through the crowd sideswiped Maddie with his suitcase. When it caught her forcefully below the knee, Maddie twisted around and lost her balance, landing in a heap on the floor. Red with embarrassment, she tried to ignore the stares from people in the crowd as her father helped her to her feet.

"Are you all right, Maddie?" asked Mr. Stoner. The worry lines around his eyes seemed to deepen.

The man with the suitcase was there too. "I'm so sorry," he said. "I hope you're not hurt."

Maddie stood up and tested her legs— they seemed okay. The rest of her did, too. She mumbled that she was fine and hurried toward her mother, who was ahead and hadn't seen her fall.

"I'm Ellen Stoner," said Maddie's mom, smiling warmly. "Are you Clive Bromley?"

The teenager nodded. He was tall with sandy hair that fell over his forehead. He wore jeans, a slightly rumpled T-shirt, and high-top sneakers.

Maddie looked around for the chalky-faced, black-clad woman who had been with Clive. She was nowhere to be seen. Maddie supposed that she must have gone to get their luggage.

Mr. Stoner came forward. "Welcome, Clive," he said. "Give me five." He held out his hand.

Clive grinned. "That must be American for 'let's shake.'" He grasped Mr. Stoner's hand. "I think I'm going to like it here."

"Good!" Mr. Stoner smiled. "Do you have

your claim ticket? We might as well collect your things and head for home."

Clive dug into the pocket of his jeans. "It's right here," he said.

"Didn't your friend go for the baggage?" Maddie asked.

Clive stared at her.

"This is Maddie," said Mrs. Stoner.

"How do you do?" Clive said formally. "What friend?"

"The tall woman in black."

Clive's eyes narrowed and shifted uneasily. "I'm alone," he said, almost too softly to hear.

"But she was walking with you," said Maddie. "She—"

"You must be mistaken, Maddie," Mr. Stoner interrupted. He turned to Clive. "Let's get your suitcases, son."

Puzzled, Maddie tagged behind as they headed toward the baggage claim area. She kept looking around for the woman in black. She peered through the knot of people gathered around the carousel. There was no one who looked like the woman she had seen with Clive. Where could she have gone in the short moment that Maddie had been on the floor? And why had Clive said that he didn't know her when Maddie was sure she had seen them together?

In the car on the way home, Maddie asked Clive about the woman again. This time, he not only insisted that he had been alone, but denied having seen any woman in black.

How could he not have noticed her, Maddie wondered, *when she was right next to him?* She was not the sort of person anyone would forget. It seemed to Maddie that Clive was uncomfortable whenever she mentioned the woman in black. His eyes darted nervously. Maddie was sure he was lying. But why?

Mr. and Mrs. Stoner were sitting in the front seat, and Maddie and Clive were in the rear. Maddie sneaked quick glances at him. What she saw wasn't bad. Not at all! Clive was definitely good-looking. He had a lean but muscular build. His face was angular and interesting, with a wide mouth and deep-set blue eyes.

One thing Clive wasn't, though, was talkative—in fact, he seemed almost shy. But he politely answered everyone's questions with a clipped English accent. Once he even initiated conversation, telling the Stoners about another teenager he had met on the plane. Someone his own age to talk to had made the trip go faster, he explained.

It was only when Maddie questioned him about the woman in black that his attitude changed. He stiffened and his eyes grew dark. And after Maddie asked about the woman in black for the third time, even her mother turned around and gave her a look. It was a look that Maddie knew well, and she didn't raise the subject again.

She tried to convince herself that she was wrong about the woman in black.

Two

THEY grilled hamburgers on the Stoners' patio for Clive's first afternoon in America, and he told them more about himself and his family. The Bromleys lived in a small seaside town called Morecambe, a few miles outside the city of Lancaster, in the northern part of England.

"Morecambe is a resort on the bay," said Clive as he bit into a french fry. "Mmm... these are super chips, Maddie!"

"Chips?" Maddie giggled. "We call them french fries."

"French fries?" Clive sampled another. "Taste like chips to me." He went on with his description of Morecambe. "In summer, people come from as far off as London to

18

spend their holidays."

"Where do they stay?" Maddie asked.

"There are three hotels, and lots of people take in summer guests," Clive replied.

"Do you?" Maddie couldn't imagine having hordes of vacationers running around the house.

Clive grinned. "Not with my mum! She'd never let strangers mess up our house. She likes everything shiny and clean."

Maddie asked about his family.

"I'm an only child," Clive said.

Like me, Maddie thought.

Clive and his parents lived in a small, two-bedroom house several blocks from the beach. Most of the people living in Morecambe served the tourist trade or worked in nearby Lancaster, where many government offices and businesses were located. Clive's father was with the government engineering services in Lancaster. Clive's mother worked two days a week at the local library and spent a lot of time tending her garden.

"Gardens are important in Morecambe," Clive told them. "My mum's roses are the biggest for blocks around."

Maddie was so entranced by Clive that she only ate half a hamburger.

"The last time I saw your mother," said Mrs. Stoner, "was just before her family left for England. We were still kids. I must have been about 11 years old, and she was a year or two older."

"And they never came back to America?" Maddie asked.

"Deborah's parents did, after they retired," said Mrs. Stoner. "By that time, Deborah had married an Englishman and settled down there."

"Mum is quite thoroughly English now," said Clive, "though everybody still calls her 'The American.'"

"Does she talk like you?" asked Maddie.

Clive shook his head. "No, she still has an American accent. But it's not as bad as yours."

Maddie laughed. In her mind, Clive was the one who spoke strangely. Clive's British accent was different from anything Maddie was used to hearing. But it was nice. He sounded like one of her favorite rock stars being interviewed on MTV.

For the most part, Maddie thought Clive's

visit might be fun after all. But she was still confused by the mysterious woman in black and Clive's reaction when she even mentioned the woman. And she couldn't help but wonder why any teenage boy would want to leave a resort town in the summer. She was just going to ask him about that when he mentioned his collection of music.

"I have everything ever recorded by Blood 'n' Guts," he said.

"Really?" Maddie was delighted. "They're one of my favorite groups. They're so cool!"

When Clive smiled, his whole face seemed to light up. Maddie had a sudden feeling that she had known him for a long time. "Do you want to go up to my room and hear my tapes?" she asked.

Soon they were sitting cross-legged on the thick shag carpeting in Maddie's room, playing tapes. Their tastes in music were surprisingly similar, except that Clive enjoyed heavy metal, which Maddie couldn't stand.

She asked Clive if he wanted to go to the pool the next day. He nodded and told her that swimming was his favorite activity. Maddie sensed that now was the perfect time to ask the question that had been on her mind all day. "Why did you come to America anyway, Clive?"

The smile slipped from Clive's face like a leaf falling from a tree, and the light in his eyes faded. His voice was suddenly so low that Maddie could barely make out the words. "My mum thought it would be good for me to get away for awhile," he mumbled.

As surely as she knew her own name, Maddie knew he wasn't telling the whole truth. But Clive's lips had closed in a tight, stubborn line, and it was obvious he didn't want to talk about it anymore.

Maddie switched on the radio and listened for the weather forecast. It was optimistic—sunny, with the temperatures expected to hit the 80s. Maddie tried to push her doubts aside. It was going to be neat to introduce her cousin from England to her friends.

* * * * *

That night, Maddie had a strange dream. She was swimming, but not in the Fairmount community pool. It looked more like Long Beach Island at the Jersey shore where the Stoners sometimes went for a summer weekend. But it wasn't that beach either—not exactly. The ocean was calmer, and there was a line of sailboats racing silently across the deep water. Maddie was wearing her new bikini. In the dream, though, the bikini was black, not white.

Except for the boaters, Maddie was the only one in the water. She glanced toward the beach and saw that it was deserted too. As she began to swim toward shore, a great black shadow appeared and the water began to churn and boil. She looked up to see a huge cloud blocking out the sun. An unnatural darkness was quickly spreading across the sky. Maddie struggled toward the beach, but no matter how hard she stroked, she never seemed to get any closer to shore.

Suddenly, some sense of danger made her look behind. The ghostly figure of a tall, bony-faced woman dressed in black was standing upon the water. With one long finger, she beckoned to Maddie, and Maddie felt herself being drawn backward. Terrified, she tried desperately to swim toward shore and safety. But it was useless. Some powerful force was pulling her toward the figure in black. Maddie knew something awful was about to happen.

"No!" She tried to scream, but nothing came out. At that moment, she woke suddenly to find that she was sitting up in bed, trembling and staring into the dark.

It was only a dream, she told herself, and she lay down again. But her heart continued to pound wildly. It was a long time before she was able to fall back to sleep.

* * * * *

The next morning was sunny and cloudless—perfect for the pool. The dream was forgotten. As soon as she was dressed, Maddie phoned Chloe and told her that she was taking her cousin to the pool.

Maddie usually rode her bike to the pool. Clive borrowed Mr. Stoner's bike, and they set off in the late morning. They had only gone a short distance when Maddie heard someone call her name.

"Hold up," Maddie said to Clive, and they braked. Tommy Willis, pedaling fast, caught up to them.

"Going to the pool?" he asked. The Willises lived across the street from the Stoners, and Tommy and Maddie had been playmates since they were toddlers. Maddie considered Tommy her buddy, second only to Chloe.

Tommy was staring at Clive. "This is my cousin, Clive," Maddie told him. "He's from England. Clive, Tommy's our neighbor."

They talked for a few minutes and then headed for the pool.

When they got there, they parked their bikes outside and looked around. The pool wasn't crowded yet. Maddie spotted Chloe talking to some kids, and she and Tommy led Clive over for introductions.

Everybody was friendly and interested in Clive. Maddie could see that they were knocked out by his accent, especially the girls. It made Maddie feel important—he was *her* cousin, after all. She spread her towel over a lounge chair in a sunny spot and took out a bottle of suntan lotion.

"I'm going to soak up some sun before I go in," she told Clive.

"Do you mind if I have a bit of a swim right away?" he asked. Maddie marveled at how polite Clive was. None of the kids she knew would have asked permission.

"Sure, go ahead." She watched Clive put down his gear, peel off his shirt, and head for the edge of the pool. Chloe danced alongside him, chattering like a sparrow.

Chloe likes him, Maddie thought. *I guess I do, too.* She began to smooth the suntan lotion onto her shoulders and watched as Clive dove into the pool, with Chloe following close behind.

Clive was a good swimmer—his strokes were strong and sure. Chloe was having a tough time keeping up. Maddie laughed. She knew that Chloe would manage, no matter how hard she had to struggle. Maddie loved Chloe, but she had to admit that her friend got a little crazy around boys.

She stretched out on her towel and noticed how good the sun felt. Tommy and the other kids had jumped in the pool, and Maddie watched lazily as they swam and horsed around. Her eyes slowly closed, and she was almost dozing when she heard a scream. She opened her eyes and sat up.

"Someone's drowning!" she heard a girl

yell. Maddie's heart began to pound. She jumped up and ran to the edge of the pool and saw that the lifeguard was pulling someone up.

"It's the English kid," Maddie heard someone say. Horrified, she watched the lifeguard drag Clive's body out of the pool.

With a shiver, Maddie instantly flashed back to her dream the night before. Had it been a warning? *Clive's dead,* she thought, *and it's my fault for bringing him here!*

Then she saw that Clive was moving. He wasn't dead. He crouched on all fours and began to cough up water. Maddie rushed over to him. "Clive! Are you okay?"

He looked up at her, still sputtering. "She pushed me!" he growled. His voice cracked and faltered. "She made me hit my head on the bottom. Nearly did me in."

Maddie glanced toward the entrance gate, which was flanked by a thick hedge of bushes. A tall figure in black was just disappearing behind them.

Three

"TELL me what really happened at the pool," Maddie urged.

She and Clive were home again, relaxing with soft drinks on the back deck. Much to Maddie's relief, Clive seemed all right.

A *near drowning*, Maddie thought. She thought about how Clive had looked crouching on the concrete beside the pool. Maddie couldn't remember ever having been more frightened. Actually, it seemed to her that Clive had recovered faster than she had! Once his head had cleared and he'd discovered that all he had was a minor bump, he had joked and acted as though nothing serious had occurred.

But now, when Maddie pressed him

again about what really happened at the pool, Clive kept his eyes fastened on the drink in his hand. "I don't know what you mean," he mumbled. "I got a little careless, that's all."

Maddie set her drink on a small glass-topped table. "Clive, I heard you tell the lifeguard that you made a clumsy dive and hit your head on the side of the pool."

"That's right."

"But that's not what you said at first!" Maddie pointed out. "That's not what you told me! 'She pushed me.' *That's* what you said. What did you mean? Who pushed you?"

Clive fidgeted. "Nobody." He spoke so softly that Maddie had to strain to hear him. He crossed his legs, then uncrossed them, then crossed them again. "No one pushed me. It was an accident. A bad dive."

Maddie tried to catch her cousin's eye—to get him to look at her directly. It was like trying to snare a butterfly. But Maddie knew how to get his attention. "I saw the woman in black," she told him.

Clive stood so suddenly that he knocked over his chair. It hit the wooden floor of the deck with a thud. Then he slammed his drink down on the table. Some of it slopped over, making a puddle. "There is no such person!" he shouted, his eyes blazing.

Maddie shrank back. Since his arrival, Clive had been soft-spoken and polite—until now. Maddie stared at him. She tried to say something, but she couldn't seem to get out any words.

Then, just as quickly as Clive's anger had flared, it faded. "I...I'm sorry," he said. He fingered the bump on his head. "Maybe I'm not feeling so good after all. A headache, you know." He tried unsuccessfully to smile. "I think I'll lie down for a while. Do you mind?"

How could Maddie object? But she wasn't satisfied. After Clive left, she sat alone for a while, worrying about the mystery that seemed to accompany her English cousin. She picked up a napkin and wiped up the puddle on the table. Clive was holding something back—something important. But what could it be? Maddie was determined to get to the bottom of what she was beginning to think of as the "Clive puzzle."

* * * * *

After dinner, Mr. Stoner took Clive to a baseball game at Yankee Stadium in New York. Maddie's mom had objected, still unsettled over Clive's accident earlier in the day. But Clive insisted that he felt fine, and Mr. Stoner was eager to see the game. So off they went.

Maddie had been invited to go along. She loved baseball, but unlike her dad, she was a Mets fan. She couldn't stand the Yankees. So no one was surprised when Maddie decided to stay home with her mom, who had never been interested in baseball.

As soon as Clive and Mr. Stoner were gone, Maddie confronted her mother. Mrs. Stoner was in the den, reading a novel. Maddie curled up in her favorite armchair and stared at her mother, wondering how to bring up what was on her mind.

Mrs. Stoner glanced up. "No TV, Maddie?"

Maddie shook her head. "I can't seem to concentrate tonight."

Her mother took the bait. "Why not?"

"I'm upset because Clive almost drowned today."

Mrs. Stoner placed a marker in her book

and set it down. "I guess you want to talk about Clive."

Maddie nodded. She decided on a direct approach. "He's not here just because his family thought that a vacation in the States would be fun for him, is he?"

"Well, that's part of it."

"But not the whole story, right?" Maddie insisted.

Mrs. Stoner sighed. "I guess not," she admitted. "But the truth is that I don't really know much more than what I've told you."

"What *do* you know?" Maddie uncurled her legs and sat up straight, eager for an explanation at last.

Mrs. Stoner settled back in her chair. "I was surprised to hear from Deborah," she said, adding quickly, "and happy, too, of course. When she asked if Clive could visit with us for a few weeks, naturally I agreed. After all, family is family."

"Did you ask why there was such a rush for a visit?" Maddie asked.

"Of course I did. Deborah didn't offer any details. She just mentioned that her son was having problems and needed to get away for a while."

"What sort of problems?"

Mrs. Stoner shrugged. "Just kid problems. Nothing important."

Maddie was disappointed. "But what about that woman in black?"

Her mother frowned. "What woman in black?"

"The one who was at the airport. I saw her again at the pool."

Maddie's mother shot her a disapproving look. "Maddie, are you letting your imagination run away with you?" She shook her head. "Who else has seen this person?"

"Well, no one," Maddie admitted. "But—"

"There, you see?" Her mother stopped her. "You're making a mountain out of a molehill. Clive was having a few problems and needed to get away for a while. And there is no woman in black."

Mrs. Stoner opened her book and smoothed back the pages. Then she looked at Maddie again. Her eyes softened. "Clive seems like a nice boy, Maddie, and he's far from home. Let's try to make him feel welcome."

"Sure, Mom," Maddie said. Her mom always saw the best in people. But Maddie wasn't satisfied. She hadn't learned much that she didn't already know—just that Clive was having "problems." That could mean almost anything. Maddie watched her mother reading again and realized that there would be no more information. If there was more to be learned, Maddie would have to learn it some other way, and on her own.

"I think I'll head upstairs," she said. "Maybe I'll watch TV for a while."

"All right, dear."

Maddie ran up the stairs and switched on her TV. Nothing was on but reruns. She turned up the volume so her mom would think she was in her room watching, then she tiptoed into the hall. She opened the door to the guest room and switched on the light.

The Stoners' guest room was not just a room for guests. Her dad called it the "spare room." Her mom called it the "study." They used it for a lot of different things.

Along one wall stood a large oak desk with a matching swivel chair. In a corner stood a portable sewing machine on a small table. It was seldom used, since no one in the family liked to sew. A small, three-drawer oak chest stood under one window. Along the opposite wall was a bed that looked like a couch most of the time. For now, the bolsters and cover had been removed and replaced with sheets and a pillow.

Clive's bathing trunks and towels were tossed on the bed. An open suitcase was on the floor. There were books and papers on the desk that Maddie had never seen there before. An oversized gray sweatshirt hung over the back of the chair.

Maddie stood in the doorway for a while. She wasn't sure what she was looking for. Her conscience told her that she shouldn't be snooping in her cousin's things. But curiosity won out over conscience and she stepped inside. She eyed the papers on the desk.

Right in the middle was a letter that Clive must have just started. His handwriting was large and sprawling. Maddie began reading. "Dear Mum and Dad," he'd written. "I miss you both a lot."

Funny how it had never occurred to Maddie that Clive might be missing his folks. She went on reading.

"The Stoners are nice, but I wish I was back in Morecambe. I know you won't believe this, but it has followed me here. No matter where I am, it seems to find me. Sometimes I feel like I'm going crazy."

Maddie stopped reading. She felt increasingly guilty, poking into someone's thoughts and feelings.

Maybe I should leave, she thought. She turned to go, but stopped when her eye fell upon another sheet of paper. This one was covered with writing. One word at the top leaped from the paper as though written in fire:

GHOST!

Maddie shivered. The skin on the back of her neck tightened as if stroked by icy fingers. She snatched up the paper. Underneath that terrifying word were several definitions. Clive must have copied them from a dictionary. Maddie nervously studied them:

the supposed disembodied spirit of a deceased person

soul or spirit separate from the body, appearing to the living as a pale, shadowy apparition

Instantly, an image of the chalk-faced, black-clad figure came to Maddie's mind. She shuddered, and read on:

a haunting memory
a faint, shadowy semblance
to haunt

There was a blank space after that, and then some lines that looked like poetry.

If a step should sound or a word be spoken,

Would a ghost not rise at the strange guest's hand?

Maddie's eyes widened, and she felt goose pimples rise on her skin. What did these strange words mean? She turned the paper over and saw that something was written on the back. Here the script was larger and darker, as though the writer had pressed the pen against the paper with great force:

Ghosts are associated with particular houses or places!

Then, below that, in shaky, wildly scrawled letters:

GHOSTS DO NOT TRAVEL! NO, GHOSTS DO NOT TRAVEL!

With shaking hands, Maddie put the paper back on the desk. She felt as though she had stepped into a dark, twisted place where everything was upside down and nothing was what it seemed. Clive appeared so nice...so *normal!* They even liked the same kind of music.

But these weren't the writings of a normal person.

Or were they? They could have been written by someone who was just plain scared.

Maddie glanced at the titles of two paperback books on the desk: *Ghosts and Poltergeists* and *Hauntings in Lancashire.* Clearly, Clive was interested in the topic of ghosts. Was it just curiosity? Again, Maddie thought of the figure in black. More than once, Clive had denied seeing her. Why?

I'd better get out of here! Maddie thought suddenly. She turned off the light and returned to her own room, then switched the TV off and began to get ready for bed. It was early, but she was worn out.

I shouldn't have gone looking in Clive's things, she told herself as she pulled off her sneakers and tossed them into a corner. She put on pajamas, washed her hands and face, and brushed her teeth. All the while, questions about her cousin hammered at her mind.

After calling out a "good night" to her mother, Maddie switched off the lamp on her night table and climbed into bed. Her dad and Clive had not yet returned from the ball game.

She closed her eyes, but sleep wouldn't come. The sounds of the night seemed magnified. Maddie listened to crickets chirping and the roar of an occasional passing car. She heard wind rustling through the leaves of the tree outside her open window.

And there was something else— something Maddie couldn't identify. It wasn't a noise at all, but a sense of a presence outside her window. Maddie's eyes flew open. Her heart pounding, she climbed out of bed, went to the window, and drew back the curtain.

A pale, thin face, clearly lit by the moonlight, was looking in at her. Black eyes bored into hers.

Four

MADDIE screamed. She stumbled once, then lunged for the door. She was so terrified she could hardly see where she was going, and almost collided with her mother in the hall. Mrs. Stoner was pale. "Maddie! What is it?"

Maddie flung her arms around her mother. "It... it... " She couldn't speak.

Her mother stroked her hair. "Shh, shh ...what's the matter?"

"Yes, what happened, Maddie?" asked Mr. Stoner as he reached the top of the stairs. Through her tears, Maddie spotted Clive behind him. They must have just returned from the ball game.

"A face... over there, at the window!"

Maddie pointed toward her room and buried her head in her mother's shoulder. "I . . . I can't look at it again. I can't," she sobbed.

Mr. Stoner strode rapidly to the window. A second later he said, "I don't see anything. There's nothing here."

"Is it possible she saw some sort of intruder?" Mrs. Stoner asked nervously.

Mr. Stoner pulled the curtain further back and peered intently in all directions. "No," he decided. "Anyone out there would need a ladder to reach this window. There's no sign of one." He turned to Maddie and said gently, "No one was outside your window, Maddie."

"There was!" Maddie insisted tearfully. "There was! It was someone with a . . . a white face—and terrible black eyes."

Mr. Stoner shook his head. "There's nothing here. Come and see for yourself."

Maddie forced herself to join her father. Trembling, she looked out into the night, and saw no one. She squinted into the dark. There was nothing but the starlit sky, tree branches slightly stirring, and dark grass and bushes below.

"But I *saw* a face!" Maddie insisted. "A

horrible face! It was right there, staring at me." She looked at the skeptical faces of her mother and father. "Don't you believe me?"

Maddie's father sighed and put his arm around her shoulders. "Of course we believe you *think* you saw something outside your window, Maddie. But the imagination can play a lot of tricks, especially at night. What you saw was probably a bird, or leaves blowing against the house. For just a moment, it looked like a face to you."

Maddie felt doubt creeping in. She stared out the window again. "You're right. There's nothing there," she admitted weakly.

"Of course not," her father said. He gave her a reassuring hug and firmly closed the window. "There. Maybe you'll feel better with the window shut."

Maddie told herself that her parents were right. She must have seen a shape or a shadow, something perfectly natural. She had only imagined that it was a face. All that stuff about ghosts had spooked her.

"I'm okay now," she told her parents. "I'm sorry I made such a big deal out of nothing."

"Don't worry about it," Mr. Stoner said. He patted her shoulder. "We've all had experiences like that." He smiled broadly. "As a matter of fact, just this evening, Clive and I thought we were watching a ball game, but the Yankees weren't really there. They let themselves get beaten seven to nothing." He laughed. "They couldn't have played worse if they were nothing but ghosts. Right, Clive?"

Clive was standing in the doorway. He was pale. His eyes were dark with fear.

He believes me, Maddie realized with a shock.

Then Clive seemed to come out of his trance. His smile was forced, but he began to joke with Mr. Stoner about the game they had just seen. Nothing more was said about Maddie's apparition. But after the others had gone to their own rooms, Maddie climbed back into bed, and she lay awake for a long time.

She *had* seen something at the window, and Clive knew that she had! Once again—and now more than ever—Maddie was convinced that there was a dark mystery about Clive that needed to be solved.

* * * * *

The next morning, Maddie awoke to the patter of rain on her window. Light filtered into the room, and Maddie stretched. The terror of the night before was gone, and she decided to put the whole business out of her mind. She switched on the radio and listened to the weather forecast. A steady rain was expected to fall all day.

Sunny summer days were the best, but Maddie didn't mind an occasional rainy one. Chloe or Tommy might come over, and they would play cards or Monopoly or video games. Sometimes she even liked to be alone and spend the day reading.

This summer was different—Clive was here. Maddie guessed she was expected to entertain him somehow. Swimming was out, of course. So what would they do all day? Right now, Maddie couldn't even call Chloe for help. Chloe was leaving with her family that morning for a two-week vacation in the Poconos.

Maddie's parents would be of no help either, since they had already left for work. Mr. Stoner owned a small accounting firm, and Mrs. Stoner worked there several days a week taking care of administrative matters.

Slowly, Maddie got dressed. She pulled on socks and wondered if people played Monopoly in England.

The problem of what to do with Clive was solved after breakfast. Tommy Willis came over. He lived just across the street, but he was sopping wet.

Maddie handed him a towel. "No pool today."

Tommy nodded. "That's for sure." He glanced at Clive, still seated at the breakfast table. "So how's it going, Clive?"

"Splendid," Clive answered.

Tommy and Maddie looked at each other and burst into laughter.

Clive looked puzzled. "What's so funny?"

Maddie tried to stop laughing. "Sorry, Clive. It's the way you answered Tommy. *Splendid.* It's just so... so..."

Tommy finished the thought. "So British."

Clive stood up and pushed in his chair. "Isn't 'splendid' a proper word in America?"

"Oh, it's proper, all right," Maddie assured him. "But no kid here would ever use it."

Clive frowned. "I'd really like to learn to speak 'American.'"

Tommy shook his head. "Oh no, Clive. We think the way you speak is just... just... splendid!"

That sent all three of them into gales of laughter. Maddie was relieved. They were going to have an okay time after all—rain or no rain.

They stayed in the den all morning, just talking. Clive wanted to learn about teenage life in America. He was looking forward to meeting some surfers, and was disappointed to learn that most were found three thousand miles away, in California.

"But there are other interesting things to check out," Tommy said. "New York is nearby."

Clive nodded. "I know. I've already been to Yankee Stadium."

"No kidding?" Tommy pumped Clive for details of the game. After ten minutes of "Yankees this" and "Yankees that," Maddie brought up some of the other things they could see in the "Big Apple," such as the Empire State Building and the Museum of Natural History.

"The Bronx Zoo," offered Tommy.

"The Staten Island Ferry," added Maddie.

"We can even visit that bloke I met on the plane," Clive said.

"*Bloke?*" Maddie repeated. She and Tommy cracked up.

"The kid who sat next to me," Clive explained. "He told me to look him up."

They agreed to speak to their parents and make arrangements to go to New York soon. Then Clive told them about London, which he had visited many times, and offered details about his friends in Morecambe. To Maddie, it sounded as though British kids were not that different from American kids. About the only obvious difference, it seemed to her, was in their accents and some of the words they used.

"I'm going to learn to speak 'American,'" Clive declared. "When I go back home, maybe I'll be able to sound as American as my mum."

Maddie and Tommy were willing to help. They told Clive that female parents in America were "Mother" or "Mom" or "Ma," but never "Mum."

"That'll be a hard one to remember," said Clive. "I've called my mother 'Mum' all my life."

"That's no problem," Maddie assured him. "When I was a little kid, I called my mother 'Mommy,' but that changed when I got older."

"Change doesn't come as easily in England as it does here," Clive said. His eyes suddenly clouded. "Things that happened long ago still influence our lives."

What a strange thing to say, thought Maddie. "What do you mean?" she asked.

"Here, everything is new," said Clive, a far-off look in his eyes. "Back home, it's the old that controls us. Sometimes there's no escape."

Maddie stared at her cousin. "No escape from what?" She shuddered at the memory of the face in her window. "Is someone after you, Clive?"

Clive seemed to return abruptly from wherever he had been. He straightened his shoulders, and his eyes cleared. "After me?" He smiled. "The only ones after me are the girls." He winked at Tommy, adding, "I wish!"

Tommy winked back. "Are English girls any different from those you've met here?"

"Forget the girls!" snapped Maddie. "What

did you mean about being controlled by the past?"

Clive shrugged. "Just...just tradition. I guess that's what I meant. We have stronger traditions in England."

Maddie didn't believe that was what Clive had meant. But he and Tommy were already comparing English and American girls and ignoring Maddie's efforts to turn the conversation around.

Tommy stayed for lunch—tuna sandwiches. Clive described fish and chips, his favorite lunch back home.

After eating, they taught Clive how to play Monopoly. In no time at all, he was playing like an expert, and ended up winning by building hotels on Boardwalk and Park Place.

Both Tommy and Maddie teased Clive, insisting that his winning was just beginner's luck.

"Maddie's the one who always wins," Tommy said. "When I play Monopoly with her, I never stand a ghost of a chance."

Maddie saw Clive stiffen at the word *ghost*.

"Do you believe in ghosts, Clive?" Maddie

asked in a quiet voice.

Clive's face darkened. "Do you?"

Maddie shrugged. "You must know more about it than I do."

"What do you mean?"

"I saw your books," Maddie told him. *"Ghosts and Poltergeists* and that other one—I don't remember its name."

Clive stared at her. "I don't know what you're talking about."

"Why did you bring books about ghosts?" Maddie persisted.

Clive was gazing over Maddie's shoulder to some point behind her. He had that *look* again—that spaced-out expression. Goose bumps scissored down the back of Maddie's neck. She whirled around quickly, half-expecting to see a dark, threatening figure. But no one was there. When she turned back, Clive was busy helping Tommy stack the Monopoly money in the box.

It was almost time for dinner when Tommy left. Maddie's parents had returned from work about an hour earlier, and Tommy called out a hasty goodbye when he realized how late it had gotten. Tommy was practically family, and already he and Clive had become buddies. They poked fun at each other and made little private jokes. Maddie was glad to see her cousin getting along so well with her friend. She was still sure that Clive had some terrible secret, but it was a relief to see that he could have a good time too, like any other kid.

*   *   *   *   *

After dinner, they settled in the den to watch TV. At about eight-thirty, Clive said he wanted to get something from his room. "I'll be right back," he told Maddie.

A situation comedy came on at nine o'clock. Maddie munched on a bag of nachos. When the episode ended a half hour later, she realized that Clive had never returned.

She went upstairs. The door to the guest room was half-opened. After a quick knock, Maddie pushed the door all the way open and peeked inside.

The room was empty. Maddie looked down the hall. No one was there. She looked in all the rooms on the second floor. They were empty, too.

Maddie ran downstairs again and searched the house. Clive was nowhere to be found. She hurried into the den, where her parents were now watching TV.

"Mom!" she yelled. "Dad! I can't find Clive anywhere. It's like he just disappeared!"

"He must be around somewhere," said Mr. Stoner. "I spotted him going upstairs not too long ago."

"But I looked!"

"Well, look again, Maddie," her mother said.

"Okay," Maddie replied. "But I know he's not there." Taking the steps two at a time, she rushed back upstairs and searched some more, calling out Clive's name. Nothing.

Maddie decided to take one final look in the guest room. She even opened the closet door and peered inside. Just before she left the room, she glanced out the window, and something caught her eye.

Clive was standing below in the backyard. *He must have slipped out through the patio door without anyone hearing him,* Maddie said to herself.

Maddie looked down, her nose pressed

against the glass. What was he doing? It was dark. The rain had stopped, but the sky was still murky. The moon and stars were hidden by clouds. There was just enough light coming from the house to make out Clive's sandy hair and profile.

Maddie squinted, trying to see more. Clive was looking at something behind the bushes. Maddie saw him gesture once. It looked like he was talking to someone, but who? As Maddie stared at the strange scene, something moved at the edge of a bush. The light was poor, but Maddie's eyes were quickly adjusting to the filmy dark. She could just make out what appeared to be a tall, thin shape.

Could it be that mysterious woman in black?

Maddie took the steps two at a time, stopping at the den to call a quick, "Never mind—I've found him," to her parents. Then she ran out to the backyard.

Clive turned at the sound of Maddie's footsteps. Even in the dark, it seemed to Maddie that his face was pale.

"Maddie?" he said.

Maddie ignored him. She poked behind

the bushes. She ran around the yard, searching every corner and looking behind each tree.

"What are you looking for?" Clive asked.

"Her!" Maddie exclaimed. "The woman in black."

"I told you before," said Clive. "There is no woman in black."

"I don't believe you!" Maddie burst out. "I saw her at the airport and I saw her at the pool. I know for sure now that it was her face looking through my window last night. And just now, I saw her out here!"

Maddie was furious. "Why are you lying?" she demanded. "Who is that woman?" Maddie recalled Clive's papers and books. "Or should I say, *what* is she?"

Clive gnawed on a fingernail. Finally, he looked up. "I'll tell you the truth—on one condition," he said softly.

"What's that?"

"That you don't tell anyone else. It must be a secret. Can I trust you?"

Maddie nodded. "I promise."

"Okay," Clive said. He took a deep breath. "The woman in black... it's the Lancaster Witch."

Five

"MAYBE it's good that you found out," Clive said solemnly, "in case anything happens to me."

They were back in the house. After a brief explanation to Maddie's parents that Clive had a headache and had gone out to get some fresh air, Maddie and Clive went upstairs. Maddie switched on the radio, which was tuned to her favorite FM station.

"We can talk in here," she said. "They'll think we're listening to music." She and Clive sat cross-legged on the rug.

"You did say *witch*, didn't you?"

Clive offered a thin smile. "Have you ever heard of the witches of Lancashire?"

"What's Lancashire?" Maddie asked. "I

thought you came from a village near Lancaster."

"Lancaster is a city," Clive explained. "It's in the county of Lancashire. So is the town of Morecambe where I live. Anyway, the witches of Lancashire are supposed to have done their evil work in the seventeenth century."

Evil? Witches? Maddie shook her head. "Honestly!" she exclaimed. "It's hard to believe that people could ever believe that stuff."

"Yes, but you have to remember that this was more than three hundred years ago," Clive said. "No one knew about germs and viruses then. When people got sick or died suddenly, they blamed it on witches."

Maddie sighed. "This is a lot different than just seeing the wicked witch in reruns of *The Wizard of Oz*."

Clive nodded. "Back in the 1600s," he continued, "people didn't like cranky old women who lived alone. Sometimes they were accused of witchcraft—and witchcraft was a crime in those days."

"What happened to them?"

"They were put on trial. If they were

found guilty, they were executed."

"But that's not right!" Maddie protested. "I mean, it's not like they were real witches!"

Clive shrugged. "Actually, some of them *were* into magic. They believed they could cast spells."

"But they couldn't, could they?"

Clive raised his eyebrows. "I don't know. They thought they could. So did their neighbors. But that wasn't the worst of it. Many of those women—mostly it was women—never had anything to do with spells or witchcraft. Maybe someone didn't like them or was jealous or trying to get even with them. Other people were too scared to help. They were afraid they might be next."

Maddie shuddered. "I'm glad I live in the good old U.S.A."

Clive stared at her. "It happened here, too. Didn't you ever hear of a place called Salem?"

Maddie shrugged. "I think so."

"It's in your state of Massachusetts. There was a witch scare there once. A lot of people were accused of being witches and executed—burned to death. So, it wasn't only in England."

Maddie looked at her cousin admiringly. "How do you know all these things? Did you learn it from those books?"

Clive nodded. "There are lots of other books, too. I've read them all. You could say that I'm an expert on witches." His tone was light, but his eyes were troubled.

"Tell me about the witches of Lancashire," Maddie urged. "What do they have to do with you?"

"In 1612," Clive said, "there was a witch panic in Lancashire. Ten women were accused of witchcraft. There was a trial and they were found guilty. All ten of them," he continued, "were hanged outside Lancaster Castle."

"Oh, gross!" Maddie rubbed her neck. She tried unsuccessfully to erase from her mind a gruesome picture—ten woman wearing black capes and hanging, all in a row.

"I still don't see what that has to do with you," Maddie said.

"One of the women was named Elizabeth . . . Elizabeth Device. She—"

"This woman, this Elizabeth Device," Maddie interrupted, "—was she one of the *real* witches?"

Clive shrugged. "I don't know. From what I've read, people believed that she was able to cast spells. She was supposed to be the head of a whole family of witches. Just before Elizabeth Device was hanged, she cursed the judge and all of his descendents."

The image of a tall, pale woman in black flashed through Maddie's mind. She was almost afraid to ask the next question. "What was the judge's name?"

Clive's eyes darkened. "Lord Bromley."

"Bromley is your last name," Maddie said in a hushed voice.

Clive's eyes met Maddie's. "I'm a direct descendent."

"Then there really *is* a woman in black!" Maddie jumped up and switched off the radio. The music was beginning to annoy her. "You've seen her!" she shouted. "I *knew* you weren't telling the truth when you said there was no such person!"

Clive looked away. "I'm sorry. I didn't want anyone here to know about her. She's the reason I had to leave Morecambe." He turned back to face Maddie. "Besides, I'm not sure that she really exists, except in my imagination."

"Haven't others in your family seen her?"

Clive shook his head. "No one else has seen her, and no one wants to talk about her." He scratched his lip. "I've heard rumors about Bromley hauntings for years, but my dad says that's a lot of superstitious nonsense."

Maddie looked sympathetically at Clive. She couldn't think of anything to say.

"About a year ago I started to see her," Clive continued. "At least, I *thought* I saw her. It's so easy to mistake a shadow or a blur for something else. And sometimes weeks go by without anything happening. But then suddenly, I'll feel something behind me. When I turn around, there's a figure disappearing behind a building or around a corner."

"I know what you mean," said Maddie excitedly. "It was the same for me at the airport and at the pool."

"And the face at your window," Clive reminded her.

"I'll never forget that!" Maddie shivered. "But I still don't see why you had to leave home."

"I knew the family history," Clive

explained. "I told my friends that I was being haunted by the ghost of Elizabeth Device. They just laughed and thought I was getting weird. After a while, I noticed that people were looking at me in a funny way. I'm sure they were talking about me, saying things like, 'There goes that strange Bromley boy who thinks he's being followed by a ghost.' That sort of thing."

"How awful," said Maddie.

"It was," he agreed. "Anyway, Mum and Dad decided it would be best to get me away from Morecambe for a while. Mum thought of her American relatives. So, here I am," Clive said.

"But she followed you here, didn't she?"

Clive shrugged. "I . . . I'm not sure. I thought I saw her a few times. Then you spoke about her too. By now, I don't know what to think."

Maddie stared at him. "Weren't you talking to her in the backyard?"

Clive blushed. "I thought I saw her behind a bush. I tried asking her to leave me alone, but I didn't see anything clearly. Just a shadow."

"What did she say?"

"Nothing. She never speaks." Clive fidgeted with his shoelaces. "The truth is, maybe everyone *is* right and I'm seeing things that aren't there."

"But I've seen the ghost, too," Maddie insisted.

Clive got up and stared out the window. "Maybe, maybe not. It *is* possible you just imagined it too. Maybe it's contagious, like those old witch scares."

Maddie shook her head. "It wasn't my imagination." But she didn't feel as certain as she sounded.

Clive turned from the window. "You won't tell anyone, will you?"

"No."

"Do you promise?"

"I promise," Maddie assured him.

Clive sighed. "Thanks, Maddie. I don't want your family and friends to think I'm crazy."

* * * * *

That night, Maddie tossed and turned in bed. Her mind churned with images of witches and ghosts. She wasn't sure what to think. She didn't know what was real and what wasn't.

Maybe Clive *was* crazy, and maybe she *was* catching it from him, the same way people caught measles or chicken pox.

Finally, Maddie fell asleep, only to awaken suddenly in the middle of the night. She sat up in bed with a creepy feeling that she was not alone. Nervously, she leaned over and switched on her bedside lamp. The light cast shadows in the dark corners of her room. Maddie's heart pounded so loudly that she thought she could actually hear it.

Reluctantly, she climbed out of bed and walked around the room, peering into corners and behind furniture. Then, just as she began to conclude she was making things up again, something caught her attention in the large mirror that hung over her dresser. She looked into it.

A pale face, long and thin, looked back at her. Dead, black eyes probed hers.

Maddie screamed. With a sharp crack, the mirror splintered. Slivers of glass bounced off Maddie's cheek and shoulders. They felt like icy fingers.

She screamed again and again. The real

world seemed to break apart along with the glass in her mirror. She clutched at her arms, her head, her chest, trying to hold on to herself. Something was pulling her into the darkness behind the looking glass.

Six

MADDIE heard muffled sounds of doors flinging open and footsteps hurrying along the hall.

"Maddie!" Her mother's voice seemed to come from a great distance. It sounded hollow, like a whisper in a tunnel.

"Maddie!" Her father was shaking her.

Slowly, Maddie felt herself being jerked back into the real world. She stared at her parents' worried faces. Farther back, in the shadows of the hall, she saw Clive. His face was white and he was chewing on a fingernail.

With a trembling finger, Maddie pointed at the mirror. Where glass remained, a web of fine cracks showed clearly. Small, jagged pieces of glass lay on the floor and on the top of the dresser.

"It was there!" Maddie croaked. She hardly recognized her own voice. "In the mirror!"

"What was there?" Mr. Stoner asked.

"The face! The same one I saw in the window."

Her parents exchanged glances. Maddie could almost hear the message being flashed on their private telegraph—*oh, no, not again.*

"Oh, Maddie," said her mother, "if you saw a face in the mirror, it was your own."

"Clive! Tell them!" she demanded, hurrying into the hall.

But Clive had managed to disappear. *The chicken!* Maddie thought. Then she remembered her promise to him. She couldn't mention the Lancaster Witch.

Maddie stumbled to the bed and sank into it, rubbing her eyes. Her father sat beside her. "Maddie," he said gently, "a nightmare can be very upsetting."

"You think I'm imagining things?" Maddie stared at her father angrily.

"I think you awoke suddenly from a bad dream and looked in the mirror. You saw your own reflection there."

"But the mirror's broken," Maddie said. "How do you explain that?"

"Easily enough," replied her father. "You were walking around your room half-asleep and stumbled into the dresser. It banged against the wall and shook the mirror, which caused the glass to crack."

Once again, everything her father said made sense. Maddie began to feel like a complete jerk. "I guess you're right," she said. "That must be what happened."

Could it be true? she wondered. *Such a simple explanation?* She had been so sure of what she had seen.

Mrs. Stoner had gotten a paper bag from somewhere. She began picking up glass from the floor. "Why don't you lie down, Maddie," she suggested. "Things will look different after a good night's sleep. Everything is fine now."

Everything is not fine, Maddie thought. But after a few more reassuring words from her parents, she put her head on the pillow. She heard them whispering about her as they left the room.

If this keeps up, Maddie thought, *they'll*

begin to think I'm bonkers. Clive had told her about the strange way people looked at him after he told them about the ghost. Now she understood what he meant.

Is Clive a little crazy? Maddie wondered. *Am I? Is there a ghost, or isn't there?*

Everything that had happened could be logically explained. Her dad was right. Clive's wild stories had made Maddie see things that weren't there. That's what must have happened. Ghosts didn't exist in real life. Witches lived only in fairy tales.

Finally, Maddie drifted into an uneasy sleep.

* * * * *

Bright morning sunshine, streaming into the room, woke Maddie hours later. The light of day made the terror of the night seem silly. Then she looked at the mirror.

It was still broken. Cracks stretched across what remained of the surface. Maddie took a deep breath, struggling against a new twinge of fear. Firmly, she told herself that it was her own clumsiness—*not* a ghost—that had done the damage.

She slipped out of bed and confronted the mirror. All that stared back was her own face, looking cracked and broken—a scrambled face to match her scrambled brains.

Maddie tore herself away from the mirror. Irritated, she headed for the shower. She turned on the water full force and opened a bottle of shampoo. Working the shampoo into her hair, she scrubbed hard in an effort to wash away any cobwebs that were still clogging her mind.

Maddie reasoned that Clive was imagining things. All those ghost books had made him soft in the head. She stepped out of the shower onto the cool tile of the bathroom floor. Clive needed her help, Maddie decided. She rubbed herself briskly with a towel, wondering what she could do. If only Chloe were around. Good ideas always came to Maddie when she talked things over with Chloe. But Chloe was away. Maddie would just have to do it alone—find some way to help her cousin.

Maddie had just finished dressing when she heard a noise—a loud cry, followed by a series of bumps. *What now?* she wondered.

She rushed into the hall and to the head of the stairs. A twisted form lay at the bottom— *Clive!*

Maddie raced down the stairs. "Clive!" she yelled. "Clive! Are you all right?" Maddie's fear returned full force.

Clive sat up slowly and rubbed his head. He tested his arms and legs. "Everything seems to be okay," he said. He pulled himself to his feet and stared at Maddie. "*She* did it!"

"Who?" As if she couldn't guess!

"Elizabeth Device. She pushed me down the stairs."

Maddie said nothing. She gripped Clive's arm and helped him to his feet. They went into the kitchen and sat down.

"Are you sure you're okay?" Maddie asked. She glanced at her watch. It was ten o'clock. Her parents would have already left for the day. "Maybe I should call my mom or dad. Or a doctor."

Clive shook his head. "I'm fine," he insisted. Then his eyes narrowed. "She wanted to hurt me."

"Maybe you just tripped."

"You don't believe me?"

"Of course I do," she assured him. "And I'm going to help. You'll see." Maddie wished she felt as sure of herself as she sounded. The truth was that she still had no idea how to go about helping her cousin.

She watched Clive carefully, still worried about the tumble he had taken. "Are you sure you're okay?" she asked.

Clive nodded. "I'm not hurt," he insisted. "See?" He got up and danced around the table. "Lucky for me your stairs have heavy carpeting. But not so lucky for *her.*"

Maddie sighed. Clive had only been there three days, and a lot of strange things had happened already. She longed for the old normal days with her normal friends.

Suddenly, Maddie had a flash of inspiration. She knew how to help her cousin. It was really simple. She could keep him busy with other things—too busy to think about the witch. Too busy to imagine he saw ghosts whenever he did something clumsy.

"You want to ride over to the pool?" Maddie asked, eager to put her new plan into operation.

Before Clive could answer, the phone

rang. It was Tommy. "I'm at the phone booth by the pool," he said. "Are you guys coming down today?"

"Hold on just a minute," she said.

Maddie laughed and turned to Clive. "It's Tommy. He must be psychic or something. He's at the pool. Should we go?"

Clive shrugged. "Why not? You don't want to spend your time talking about witches and ghosts."

Maddie ignored the sarcasm in his voice. "We'll be there right away," she said into the phone. Then she and Clive got changed and rode their bikes over to the pool.

Once there, Maddie tried to distract herself with her friends. She told herself that she had buried her fears. And with each hour that passed, her conflicting feelings did seem to fade a little more. It was nice at the pool. People were laughing and splashing and having fun. Maddie watched Clive. He seemed to be having a great time too. There was no mention of witches or ghosts or mysterious women in black.

It *had* been a good idea to go to the pool. Maddie smiled. She was beginning to feel more like her old self. Spooks and goblins didn't seem real surrounded by everyday summer sounds. It was great. Even Clive acted as though he had forgotten the bad way the day had started. And by the end of the day, when nothing else unusual happened, Maddie even convinced herself that nothing else would.

* * * * *

The next morning, Maddie noticed that two of her library books were due. Clive went with her to the library. "You can pick out some books too," Maddie suggested. "We'll take them out on my card."

Maddie found two mysteries that looked good. But she shook her head when she saw the books that Clive had chosen. They were about ghosts and hauntings.

They didn't discuss the books, and Maddie forgot about them altogether when she and Clive went to the pool again. This time, it was Clive's idea.

"I'm extremely fond of swimming," Clive told her. Maddie smiled, still tickled by the way he talked. Of course, it seemed to her that he was also fond of the way the girls followed him around. She didn't mind a bit. She was content to simply trail along, making sure he kept busy. *I really am helping him,* she thought happily.

But every now and then, while Maddie was floating lazily on her back in the water, she thought she glimpsed a tall, black figure outside the pool gate. One time she was almost sure of it. Her heart began to beat faster. She swam swiftly to the edge of the pool to get a better view. But it was just an ordinary person passing by—a bald man wearing a black turtleneck. *Definitely not a ghost,* Maddie chuckled to herself.

In the afternoon, Tommy came over and they all went for a bike ride. They rode to the civic center and past the town hall. Maddie and Tommy led Clive through the fancier parts of town and past a new shopping mall. Then they pedaled down some shabbier streets toward the edge of town. Beyond that were blocks of factories and warehouses.

Maddie pointed out an abandoned building. "That used to be a factory for the Army," she said. "They made bullets and grenades and stuff like that during the Korean War."

"It's been closed for years," Tommy added.

They pedaled closer. The grounds were overgrown with weeds, and a fence that had once enclosed the property had fallen over. Debris was scattered throughout the dead, brown grass. The building's paint was peeling, and most of the windows were cracked or boarded up.

Maddie suddenly slowed down. "What's that?" she yelled.

Clive and Tommy braked to a stop. "Where?"

"Over there." Maddie pointed toward the far end of the factory.

The boys peered. "I don't see anything," said Tommy, blinking.

"What do you see, Maddie?" asked Clive.

Maddie shook her head, annoyed with herself. "Nothing."

"It must have been something," Clive said.

"Nothing . . . it's nothing," she said uneasily. "I just imagined it." Maddie wanted to forget the whole thing.

"Imagined *what*?" Clive insisted.

"I thought I saw someone near the far

end of that building."

"Who?" Clive asked.

Maddie stared at her cousin. "A woman in black."

Clive didn't say another word. But Tommy insisted on riding around the building. Of course, no one was there.

"I told you I was imagining something," said Maddie. "The sun was in my eyes."

Clive's face was dark and unsmiling. Maddie wished that she had kept her big mouth shut! She wanted to help Clive, and here she was making things worse!

Neither of them brought it up again.

* * * * *

Maddie didn't feel well the next morning. When she went to breakfast, her stomach turned at the sight and smell of food. Before long, she returned to her room to lie down. Her mother followed her upstairs.

"It looks like you've caught a virus of some sort," said Mrs. Stoner with a sigh. "I've heard that one is going around. Fortunately, it's supposed to pass quickly."

"Great," Maddie mumbled. She closed her

eyes and went to sleep.

Maddie spent most of that day in bed. Luckily, her mom was home from work. She brought Maddie some juice to sip through a straw. Maddie got started on one of the mystery books she had borrowed from the library.

In the afternoon, Clive peeked in. "How are you feeling?"

"A little better," Maddie told him.

"If you don't mind, I'm going out for a bike ride with Tommy," Clive said. He was wearing a T-shirt and faded jeans cut off at the knees. He was starting to look like a regular American kid.

"Have fun," Maddie replied, and she went back to her book. It helped keep her mind off the way she felt.

By late afternoon, Maddie felt well enough to move around again. She went downstairs to the kitchen table and watched her mom prepare dinner. Looking at food no longer made her feel queasy.

They gossiped about things Maddie had heard at the pool until the doorbell interrupted them. It rang and rang, as though someone were leaning on it.

"We're coming!" Maddie and her mother both hurried to the front hall. Maddie got there first and yanked the door open.

Tommy was standing outside. His bike was tossed down on the sidewalk. His face was flushed.

"What is it, Tommy?" Mrs. Stoner asked.

"It's . . . it's Clive," Tommy stammered.

Maddie peered down the street. "What do you mean? Where is Clive?" she asked. "Why isn't he with you?"

"That's just it!" Tommy said. "He's gone! Something's happened to him!"

Seven

"WE were racing our bikes—Clive and me." Tommy spoke breathlessly. His words tumbled over each other. He told them how Clive had been slightly ahead when Tommy's bike buckled. "I noticed that my chain was loose, so I pulled over to fix it. Clive raced on, went around a corner and disappeared."

Tommy's voice faltered. "At first, I . . . I wasn't worried," he said. "I figured it would only take a few minutes to adjust the chain."

Tommy said that after it was fixed, he had quickly pedaled on. "I was sure I'd catch up right away," he said. He explained that he had turned the same corner that Clive had, expecting to see his new friend ahead.

When he didn't see Clive, he rode for a few more blocks. Then he saw Clive's bike on the side of the road. He said he yelled Clive's name and looked everywhere, but couldn't find him.

"I waited awhile, and then I came back here," Tommy told them. He looked miserable. "I thought maybe Clive took a different street home."

"He wouldn't have done that," Maddie said. "He doesn't know his way around well enough." She struggled not to cry.

Mrs. Stoner put a hand on Maddie's shoulder. She offered a weak smile to Tommy. "Don't worry. We'll find Clive. Tommy, just show us where he left his bike."

They decided to walk instead of taking the car. That way, there would be less chance of missing Clive if he was wandering around. Maddie and her mother hurried with Tommy to the place where Clive had disappeared. The closer they got, the more sure Maddie was that the witch of Lancaster was to blame. She shivered, even though the day was hot.

The bike was on the side of the road, just as Tommy had described. It was on a block with huge, old homes on large lots. The three of them searched all along that street and others nearby, calling Clive's name.

They climbed up to the old-fashioned front porches and rang doorbells, but few people were home. At the houses where someone did open up, no one had seen or heard anything that would lead them to Clive. It was as though he had simply vanished.

"We'd better notify the police," said Mrs. Stoner, no longer able to conceal the worry in her voice. Tommy righted Clive's bike and walked it back with them. As they all went into the house, Mrs. Stoner shook her head. "I don't know what's going on. First, Maddie imagining things. Now, Clive disappearing."

"I wasn't imagining things!" Maddie could no longer keep her fears to herself. "I know what happened to Clive."

They were in the front hall near a small table where the telephone sat. Mrs. Stoner shot Maddie an astonished look.

"It's Elizabeth Device!" Maddie blurted out. "She's done something to Clive!"

"Elizabeth Device?" Mrs. Stoner looked puzzled. "I don't recognize the name. Does she live in the neighborhood?"

Maddie didn't know whether to laugh or cry. Her mother thought Elizabeth Device was a neighbor down the block. "She's not a person, Mom," Maddie explained. "She's a ghost!"

At that moment, Maddie's father came home from work. He stepped into the hall and looked questioningly at the three worried faces. "What's this about a ghost?" he asked. "Maddie, what's going on with you now?"

Despite their skeptical expressions, Maddie told Tommy and her parents about the witches of Lancashire. She quickly related everything she could remember from Clive's story.

Mr. Stoner set down his briefcase and took off his jacket.

"Witches? Ghosts?" He shook his head and sighed. "Come on, Maddie. What's this really all about?"

"It's *serious*, Dad! Clive is missing!"

Mrs. Stoner quickly brought her husband up to date.

A second after she finished, Mr. Stoner picked up the phone. "If Clive is missing, it's not because of any ghost. I'm calling the police." He dialed quickly. The others listened to him argue with someone at the other end. Finally, he hung up.

"The police won't do anything today," he told them. "They said that most kids who run away usually return within twenty-four hours."

"Clive is not a runaway!" Maddie said angrily.

Her father nodded. "He's probably just lost," he agreed. "I'll go out and look for him myself."

But an hour later, Mr. Stoner was back without Clive. "I guess we don't have any choice but to wait," he said, his voice strained and weary. He turned to Tommy. "You'd better go home now, Tommy, before your folks think you're lost, too."

Tommy nodded. Before he left though, he pulled Maddie into another room where her parents couldn't hear them. "Did you really mean that stuff?" he asked her. "About ghosts and witches?"

Maddie nodded fiercely. "No matter what anyone says, I know that Elizabeth Device has done something to Clive."

Tommy shook his head. "I'll come by in the morning," he said.

Friday morning, he rang the bell at seven o'clock. No one was sleeping at the Stoner house. They had been awake most of the night. About ten minutes earlier, Mr. Stoner had called the police again. Twenty-four hours hadn't passed, but after a lot of discussion, the police agreed to send a detective over.

The man who arrived a few minutes later introduced himself as Lieutenant Carlin. He didn't look at all like Maddie's idea of a detective. He was of medium height, slim, and dressed in a neat blue shirt over jeans. He had a thin yet soft-featured face, and behind oversized, rimless glasses, his eyes were brown and calm.

"Okay, I've got some notes already. But tell me about this boy again, in your own words." Lieutenant Carlin took out a notebook and pen from his pocket.

Maddie's parents recited all the information they could about Clive, his parents, and his visit to America. Maddie noticed that they didn't mention the Lancaster Witch.

"I hate to alarm Clive's parents, but shouldn't we notify them at this point?" Mrs. Stoner asked.

"Why don't you give it a few more hours?" the detective suggested. "I know this seems very unusual to you, but it happens all the time. He slipped the notebook into his pocket. "After all, Clive is a stranger here. My guess is that he just got lost. He's probably embarrassed to call and say he can't find his way back. No sense throwing his parents into a panic."

Lieutenant Carlin assured them that he'd call later that day. Then he left.

Maddie looked at Tommy. His eyes were bloodshot, as though he hadn't gotten much sleep. "I'm such a moron," he told Maddie. "I shouldn't have let Clive out of my sight."

"I'm the jerk," Maddie said, "not you. I didn't believe him about the ghost, even after I'd seen it with my own eyes."

Tommy gave her an odd look, but said nothing.

They waited. Mr. Stoner called his office to say he wouldn't be in that day. Minutes stretched into hours. When the phone rang, they all jumped. Mrs. Stoner took the call.

The conversation was short. When she hung up, her expression told them the news was bad.

"The police haven't been able to find Clive." She picked up the phone again. "Much as I hate to, I'm going to place an overseas call to Morecambe and notify his parents."

Afterward, Mrs. Stoner said that was the hardest call she had ever made. She rubbed her forehead. "I hope I never have to do anything like that again." She sighed. "The Bromleys are taking the next available flight to New York."

About an hour later, Lieutenant Carlin arrived. He, too, looked worn out. He asked Tommy to describe everything all over again.

"Did you notice anything suspicious?" the detective asked.

"What do you mean?" asked Tommy.

"Did you see anyone hanging around, or anything out of the ordinary before or during your bike ride?"

Tommy frowned. "Well, there was this car."

All heads jerked toward Tommy. Lieutenant Carlin pulled out his notebook.

"What car? Where?"

"It was parked down the block," Tommy said. "I only noticed it because I'd seen the same car a few times lately. I wondered why people would park a car and just sit there."

Lieutenant Carlin's pen scratched rapidly. "Describe the people."

Tommy shrugged. "All I saw were a couple of guys, I think." He scratched his head. "I didn't really pay much attention."

Lieutenant Carlin put away his notebook and pen. "Would you mind coming down to headquarters with me? To look at some mug shots?"

"Sure," Tommy agreed.

Headquarters? Maddie jumped up. "Can I come too?" She didn't suppose that photos of witches or ghosts were included in police department files. It was a waste of time. But she had to feel like she was helping.

Headquarters was noisy and buzzing with activity. An angry couple were complaining that their car had been stolen from a local mall. A young woman with long, straggly hair was sitting on a bench crying. Lieutenant Carlin took Tommy and Maddie to a table in a quiet corner. Sheets of photographs were spread on it.

"Look these over very carefully," he told Tommy. "Point out any faces that might seem even a little bit familiar." He glanced at Maddie. "You too, Maddie. Someone may have had an eye on Clive for awhile."

Maddie examined the photos without much interest. She knew that none of this had anything to do with Clive's disappearance. They should be looking for a tall ghost in black. Of course, Maddie's parents hadn't said a word to the police about the witch. A few times Maddie almost did. But she didn't think that anyone would believe her, especially the police. She watched Tommy leaf through the mug shots on the table. Suddenly Maddie recognized a face. It was a photograph she had just glanced at and put aside. She picked it up again.

"Do you know him?" asked the lieutenant, who had been watching carefully.

"I'm not sure," Maddie said slowly. She examined the picture. It showed a stocky, balding man. "There's something familiar about this man." She hesitated. "I think I've seen him. But I can't remember where."

The detective grabbed the photo and showed it to Tommy. Tommy shook his head. "I don't know him."

Lieutenant Carlin pushed the picture in front of Maddie again. "Try to remember," he urged. "Where did you see this guy?"

Maddie struggled to remember, but couldn't. "I don't know," she told the detective. "I can't remember. I'm sorry."

"Don't be sorry," Lieutenant Carlin said kindly. "This is the first lead we've had. You may have put us onto something important."

Maddie didn't believe that. The police had no clues. They had no idea where to find Clive. Their activities reminded her of a phrase she had once seen in a book: *whistling in the dark.* That's what the police were doing. But Maddie knew something they didn't. As soon as they arrived home, she persuaded Tommy to go out with her.

"We're going for a walk," she called to her parents.

"Stay within sight!" Mrs. Stoner called back.

Once outside, Maddie told Tommy what she wanted to do. "Forget about mug shots," she informed him. "It's Elizabeth Device we need to look for."

Tommy started to argue, but she cut him short. "If we can find that witch," Maddie said firmly, "that's where we'll find Clive."

Eight

"COME on!" Maddie urged.

Tommy closed the Stoners' front door behind him, but he lingered, his hand still on the knob.

"Well?" Maddie prodded. "Let's go!"

"There's something I've got to tell you first." Tommy seemed glued to the door.

"What?" Maddie asked. She glared impatiently at her friend.

"About this witch...this ghost... whatever..." Tommy fidgeted. He looked at his shoes, the grass, the flagstone path— anywhere except at Maddie.

"You're not coming with me!" Maddie shouted accusingly. "That's it, isn't it? You're too scared!" Everybody was letting everyone else down. She hadn't backed up Clive, and he was gone. Now Tommy was chickening out on her.

"I *am* going with you," Tommy said. "It's just that . . . well, you might as well know that I don't believe any of that seventeenth century witch stuff."

Maddie turned away stiffly. "I don't need you, Tommy. I can find Clive by myself."

Tommy released the doorknob and hurried after Maddie. "Wait a minute . . . wait a minute! I didn't say I'm not coming, Maddie. I just don't believe in ghosts. And yes, I *am* scared. But not of dead witches."

Maddie wheeled around. "What *are* you afraid of?"

"Living criminals," he replied. "We don't know who's mixed up in this. You saw what those mug shots looked like. I'm not going to let you go off alone poking your nose around. You could get hurt!"

Maddie bit her lip. Criminals had nothing to do with anything. Why wouldn't anyone listen to her? She forced herself not to yell at him though. Tommy could be of help even if he didn't think the witch existed.

"So, you're coming with me?" she asked

as calmly as she could.

"Sure! I just wanted you to know how I feel about all this ghost stuff."

"Then let's get started," said Maddie. "I think we should look for Clive in all the places where I've seen Elizabeth Device."

Tommy groaned when she used the name of the witch. Maddie ignored him. "We'll start with the closest spot—my backyard."

They walked to the rear of the house. It was almost noon. The grass glistened under a bright midday sun, and twigs crunched beneath the soles of their sneakers. Maddie poked behind trees and bushes, Tommy close behind. They searched through the shrubs that separated their yard from the one next door.

"Clive!" Maddie called. "Clive, can you hear me?"

There was nothing but silence.

"How about the shed?" Tommy suggested.

A small green shed stood near the garage. Tommy pulled the door open and they peered inside. Tools hung from holders on the wall. A lawn mower was propped up on one side. Next to it were bags of fertilizer and grass seed. No one was there.

"Let's ride over to the pool," said Maddie.

"You saw the, er . . . ghost at the pool?"

Maddie shrugged. "I thought I did once. It's worth a look." She opened up the garage and wheeled out her bike. "Anyway, it's closer than the airport."

Tommy gasped. "You saw her at the airport, too?"

Maddie nodded briskly. "Get your bike," she said.

If Tommy minded her bossy behavior, he didn't show it. He crossed the street and got his bike from his house, and the two of them rode to the pool. It was closed. One day each week the pool didn't open until two-thirty in the afternoon, and then it remained open till nine. At this time of day, no one was around yet—not even the guards. Maddie tried one of the gates. It was locked.

"We can climb the fence," she said, eyeing the chain link fence that enclosed the pool. It didn't look too high. Maddie clambered up and over. Tommy followed. Inside the pool area there weren't many places to hide. They looked behind bushes and peered into the locked refreshment stand. They checked the restrooms.

Tommy nudged Maddie. "Let's get out of here. We'll be in major trouble if anyone finds us."

Maddie agreed, and they climbed back over the fence.

Tommy scratched his head. "I don't know about the airport, Maddie. "We'd never get there on our bikes."

Maddie chewed on her lip, trying to remember every spot where she had glimpsed the ghost of Elizabeth Device. "There's one more place close by where I've seen her," she finally said. "It's not far from here."

They rode their bikes to the part of town where the warehouses and factories were located.

"Isn't this where we came with Clive the other day?" Tommy asked as they passed a factory.

"Yes." The sign on the building read, "BOUTIQUE BUTTONS." They could hear the clatter of machinery and the sounds of voices inside. Maddie slowed down and pointed to a building a short distance ahead. "I think I might have seen Elizabeth Device there, by that old abandoned factory."

Maddie glanced at Tommy's face. He rolled his eyes, but said nothing. They pedaled the rest of the way in silence. They rode right over the broken-down fence and struggled to steer their bikes through the overgrown weeds surrounding the factory grounds.

Suddenly, Maddie braked and pointed. "Look!"

Tommy skidded to a halt beside her. "Where?"

"There! Up ahead," Maddie yelled. "Along the side of the building. I think I saw someone go around to the back."

Tommy held a hand over his eyes to reduce the glare of the sun. "I don't see anything."

"Come on." Maddie jumped off her bike, letting it fall into the weeds. She set off at a run, and Tommy raced behind her.

Maddie stopped when she came to the corner of the building where she had seen the figure. She stepped cautiously around to the back.

"There's no one here," said Tommy. "We ought to—"

"Look!" Maddie pointed. "There she is

96

again!"

A tall dark figure, its face cloaked in shadows, watched them from the far end of the building. It slipped quickly around another corner, and out of sight.

The Lancaster Witch!

"Did you see her?" Maddie demanded.

Tommy blinked rapidly. "I . . . I don't know. I'm not sure."

Maddie grinned. Tommy had seen the ghost. She knew it. "She's here, Tommy! Clive must be nearby." Maddie tried to concentrate on her cousin and not think about the terror she felt.

"Why does she keep disappearing around corners?" Tommy asked. His eyes were wide and confused.

"I don't know." Maddie was already striding toward the corner where she had seen the dark figure. Tommy followed close behind. "It's almost as though she's trying to *lead* us somewhere."

"That's ridiculous," said Tommy. But he sounded less sure of himself. They rounded the corner. This time, there was no one and nothing in sight. They stared at the rundown factory.

"Listen. What's that?" asked Maddie, tilting her head.

"What?"

"I thought I heard noises coming from that building."

"It's closed," Tommy reminded her. "No one ever goes inside."

The sounds came again. This time they were louder. "You're right!" said Tommy. "I hear voices."

"Yeah, and they're coming from the factory," Maddie whispered. "Let's look inside." She pointed to a window a few feet away. It was partially boarded up.

"We'd better be quiet," Tommy warned. "I don't like this."

Maddie knew he was thinking of the tough faces he had seen in the photos at the police station.

They walked carefully along the outside wall until they reached the window. Then they peered through a space between the boards.

Two men stood only a few feet away, their backs toward the window. They were smoking cigars and talking in low, muffled voices.

Tommy and Maddie ducked down quickly. When her heartbeat had slowed a little, Maddie whispered, "Let's take another look." They stood up and once again peeped cautiously between the boards. One of the men was gesturing. Cigar smoke spiraled toward the ceiling in wispy gray puffs. Peering through the smoke, Maddie could just make out a third person in the room, someone seated on a chair in the far corner. He, too, had his back to the window.

Maddie squinted, leaning forward as close as she dared. The person in the chair was tied with ropes that went around the chair slats. With a jolt, Maddie realized it was Clive. She grasped Tommy's arm, pulling him to the ground.

"Did you see Clive?" she asked anxiously, trying to keep her voice low. "They've got him tied up!"

Tommy nodded. Maddie pulled him along the side of the building, until they were a safe distance from the window.

"Did you notice the big bald guy?" Maddie whispered.

"Yeah."

"He looks like the man I identified at the

police station."

Tommy shook his head. "I don't get it. Why would they do this to Clive?"

"I don't know," said Maddie, "but we've got to get him out of there." She jumped up.

Tommy pulled her back down. "Wait a minute, Maddie! We've got to have a plan," he whispered. "We can't just go rushing in."

They crouched in silence, wondering what to do. Then Maddie touched Tommy's arm. "I've got an idea." Quickly, she outlined a plan.

Tommy looked doubtful. "You really think it will work?"

Maddie shrugged. "Can you think of anything better?"

Practical as always, Tommy suggested they go to the police.

"We can't waste the time!" Maddie said. "What if they're gone by the time the police get here? Then we'll have lost Clive again. No, we're here now, and we've got to get him out."

Tommy shuffled uneasily. "All right," he agreed. "But let's go over the plan one more time."

They discussed it again. Tommy came up

with a few suggestions in case anything went wrong. Finally, they were ready. At Maddie's signal, Tommy nodded and moved away.

Crouching low, Maddie tiptoed through the scratchy weeds until she was beneath the window. She waited. Her hands trembled. Her whole body was tingling.

A few seconds later, Maddie heard the sound she was waiting for—a loud banging. It was Tommy. He had gone around to the front of the building and was pounding on the door.

Quietly, Maddie pulled herself up just high enough to peer inside. Both men were looking toward the door. They seemed to be arguing. Maddie scrunched forward to risk a closer look.

One man was stout and middle-aged. He had a large face and a round, balding head. It *was* the man she had identified at the police station. And now Maddie knew where she had seen him before. He had been lurking by the pool just the other day. Maddie searched her memory. Somewhere else, too. She had a fleeting image of the airport and the man's face in the crowd.

Maddie strained to hear what they were saying. She could pick out some of their conversation.

"I'll go see what's happening," the bald man said gruffly. He went into the hall and was soon out of sight.

The other man paced nervously, puffing on a cigar. He was small and wiry, with greasy black hair. He had a thin, cruel face, and eyes like a hawk. He glared at Clive, then at the hall through which the bald man had disappeared.

Maddie's heart sank. If the thin man didn't leave, the whole plan would fall apart.

The banging on the door continued. But it sounded more urgent, and then Maddie heard Tommy's voice shouting, "Fire! Fire!"

The man threw another dark look at Clive, tossed down the cigar, and strode out of the room.

Now was the time to move! Maddie's legs felt even weaker than when she had been in bed with the virus. She had to force herself to stand. After taking a second to catch her breath, she ripped away some of the loose, rotting boards that covered the window. Ignoring the jagged splinters, she climbed up and scrambled inside and dashed to where Clive sat, bound and gagged.

His eyes widened. Maddie gave him a quick, worried smile, and then quickly tore away the tape that covered his mouth. His eyes watered at the flash of pain, and Maddie winced, but she wasted no time. She immediately began to fumble with the ropes.

"Maddie!" he cried. "How—?"

"Shh!" Maddie put a finger to her lips and pointed toward the hall. "There's no time now."

She picked furiously at a tight knot in the rope that bound Clive's wrists, picking and pulling desperately. Through the open window, she could hear angry shouts outside and the sound of running feet.

Tommy! Maddie prayed that the men wouldn't catch up with him, reminding herself that Tommy was a fast runner. His ability to race had been an important part of their plan.

Finally, Maddie managed to pull the knot loose. As soon as Clive's hands were free, he helped untie the other ropes. In a few seconds he was free.

"Let's get out of here!" Maddie whispered.

They struggled out the window. In the distance, they saw three figures running. The smaller one in front was Tommy and he was far ahead.

"Good work, Tom!" Maddie whispered. At that moment, the bald man turned around. He must have seen Maddie and Clive, because he yelled something and began to run back toward the factory. Maddie pulled at Clive's sleeve. "Come on! We've got to get out of here," she said. "Let's go the other way."

They tore through the deserted yard and around the opposite side of the building. The tall weeds caught at their ankles, but they managed to reach the far end, raced to the nearest street, and cut across.

Once out of sight of the building, they stopped to rest. The bald man was nowhere in sight.

"I think we lost him," Maddie said, panting. "But now we have to figure out where Tommy went. He was supposed to find a place where he could get help." She looked around uncertainly.

"Look!" Clive pointed toward the far end of the block.

They both saw her clearly. It was the Lancaster Witch. She hung there eerily, tall and thin, her feet several inches off the ground. A wide cape swirled around her like vampire wings. The whiteness of her long, bony face gleamed above the blackness of her clothes. Her eyes burned like twin lumps of coal.

Nine

THE Lancaster Witch beckoned to them.

Clive's face turned white. "It's her," he whispered.

The apparition extended one black-draped arm. A bony finger pointed.

"She's telling us to go around that corner," said Maddie.

"No way!" Clive's voice trembled. "Whichever way *she* points, I'm going in the opposite direction."

"She helped us find you," Maddie told him.

Clive's eyes narrowed. "I don't believe it."

"It's true!" Maddie insisted. She glanced around nervously. "Look, those guys might catch up to us any second." She looked fearfully at the figure ahead. It was as still as a statue, its arm and finger frozen in place. Maddie shivered. But she made herself moved toward the ghost. "Come on!"

Reluctantly, Clive moved forward and caught up with her. The witch nodded and disappeared around the corner.

"I don't trust her," Clive muttered. When they rounded the corner, they saw the witch again. Now she was pointing to a large building on the next block. Clive and Maddie hurried on. But as they neared the point where the witch stood, there was a sudden *pop*, and she was gone. Nothing remained except a heaviness in the air.

"I think she was showing us that factory down the street," Maddie said, panting. "Let's hurry." They raced to the next block. Maddie gestured at a sign on the stone wall of the building. "This is the other side of the button factory."

They ran up a walkway that led from the street to a small red door. Clive tried the knob, but the door didn't budge. "It's locked!" Clive said. Maddie banged on the door a few times.

"Maybe it's a fire exit and it opens only

from the inside," Clive suggested. They looked at each other, not sure what to do next.

"There's a big door on the other side," Maddie recalled. "It must be the way in." They hurried back to the street and turned the next corner. Halfway down the building was an entrance. "Maybe this is where Tommy went," Maddie said hopefully.

They passed through a gate into the yard and ran toward the door. A small knot of people were gathered just inside the entrance.

In the middle was Tommy!

"Tommy!" Maddie pushed her way through. The workers stood aside to let her and Clive pass.

"It worked!" Tommy exclaimed. Perspiration clung to his cheeks and forehead. "You made it!"

"I saw those men following you," said Maddie. "One of them looked as if he was getting close."

Tommy nodded. "He was! Man, was I scared! Those guys mean business. But then I remembered this place was pretty close. I ran faster than I ever have before. They didn't dare follow me inside."

Maddie nudged Clive with her elbow. "Nobody can run as fast as Tommy. He's sure to make the track team."

Tommy smiled broadly. "That was our plan, Clive. I got those guys to follow me so that Maddie could get you out of there."

Maddie looked toward the entrance. "Where are they now?"

"I think one of them turned back," said Tommy. "The other just faded out of sight when I came in here."

Maddie felt a stab of fear. "Then they might still be hanging around." The words stuck in her throat. "Waiting for us."

The workers had been listening. One of them, a tall man with glasses and a kind face, came forward. "Don't worry. Your friend told us what happened. We won't let anybody get near you."

A large woman with plump red cheeks put her arm around Maddie. "You're perfectly safe now, honey. We called your parents and the police. They should be here in a few minutes."

Clive looked from Maddie to Tommy. "I still don't quite understand. How were you able to find me?"

Tommy looked around cautiously. He pulled Maddie and Clive to a corner where they couldn't be overheard. "Maddie's the one," he whispered. "Nobody believed what she said about the witch. But Maddie kept insisting that if we found her, we'd find you too."

Clive's eyes lit up. "Then *you* saw her, too?" he asked Tommy eagerly. "You saw the witch?"

Tommy made an impatient face. "I guess so," he mumbled.

Clive grinned. "I'm glad you found me. But you were wrong. The witch had nothing to do with this."

"What did happen?" Tommy asked.

"Yeah," Maddie searched her cousin's face. "Who are those guys? What did they want?"

Before Clive could respond, a man in the crowd called to them. "Hey, kids. Someone's here for you."

Maddie's parents were coming through the door. Lieutenant Carlin was right behind them.

Maddie's mother rushed in. She flung her

arms around her daughter. "Oh, Maddie! Are you okay?" Her face showed worry, anger, relief, and joy. "How could you do such a foolish thing? Running off to play detective! This isn't one of those mystery books you're always reading. This is real!" She hugged Maddie even tighter, then looked at Tommy and Clive. "Clive! We've been looking for you everywhere!"

Mr. Stoner came forward. He put one arm around Tommy and the other on Clive's shoulder. "Why don't we get these kids home and leave the explanations for later?" He turned to the detective. "Can we take them home, Lieutenant?"

Lieutenant Carlin nodded. "I guess so. I'll come by later to question them. First I want to look around."

"You've got to find those blokes who grabbed me," Clive said. "They were holding me in that old building on the next block." He gave Lieutenant Carlin a description of the two men.

"We'll find them," the detective assured him. He waved the Stoners and the three kids ahead. "Go on now. I'll see you soon."

Once everyone settled into the car, the

questions came fast and furious.

"The whole thing was a mistake," Clive said.

"A mistake?" asked Mr. Stoner.

Clive nodded. "I knew there had to be some mistake as soon as they grabbed me off the bike and stuffed me into their car."

"You must have been terrified!" said Maddie.

"I was," Clive admitted. "I couldn't believe what was happening. Who would want to kidnap me? Mum and Dad aren't even rich."

"Did you tell the kidnappers that?"

"Of course I did. They didn't pay any attention at first. Just drove to that spooky old factory and tied me to a chair."

Mr. Stoner's voice was tight with anger. "I'd like to get my hands on those creeps."

"I wish you could!" said Clive. Then he continued his story. "They started asking me a lot of questions. They thought I had something that belonged to them."

"Like what?" Maddie asked.

"A package. I got the impression that it was worth a lot of money."

"What kind of package? What was in it?"

Clive shrugged. "I don't know, but they

were furious. They were sure I was hiding it from them."

"Even when you told them they had made a mistake?"

"They wouldn't believe me," said Clive. He frowned and shook his head. The car pulled into the Stoners' driveway, and Mr. Stoner turned off the engine. But nobody made a move to get out.

"Did they hurt you?" asked Mrs. Stoner softly.

"They punched me around a little." Clive put his hand up to his cheek. There was a red blotch there. His lip looked swollen, too. "The little guy kicked me once." He touched his arm gingerly, and winced. "Then one of them—the fat guy—said something about following me from the airport."

"I knew it!" cried Maddie. "I was right! I *did* see him at the airport. I *knew* it!"

"They've been following me ever since I got here," Clive said. "That's when I realized what must have happened."

"What?" Tommy asked.

"They were following the wrong kid. I figured it out as soon as the fat bloke said they saw me at the airport. It must have been the other kid they wanted."

"What other kid?"

"The other teenage lad. He was sitting next to me on the plane. You must remember, Maddie. I told you all about him."

"The kid you wanted to visit in New York?"

"That's right. He's the same age and size as I am. Even his hair is almost the same color. Those guys followed the wrong bloke."

"Did you tell them that?"

Clive nodded. "Yes. Of course, I wouldn't let on what the other lad's name is. I pretended not to know."

"Why didn't they let you go?"

"They were waiting to hear from someone they called 'the boss.'"

Maddie shuddered. "Maybe they wouldn't have let you go at all."

"That's what I was afraid would happen," said Clive. "I think they were starting to believe me, but there was no way I could be sure. And I definitely couldn't be sure what kind of instructions they would get from that 'boss.' You can imagine how glad I was to see you."

"But, Clive," Maddie began, "that

package. What do—"

Mrs. Stoner interrupted. "Let's go inside, kids. We have to phone Clive's parents and tell them he's okay."

The call caught the Bromleys at home just as they were leaving for the airport. Mrs. Stoner spoke for quite awhile. Then Clive got on the phone to reassure them that he was okay.

"Mum and Dad wanted to come anyway," Clive told Maddie later, "even after I convinced them I was fine. It took me forever to persuade them to cancel the plane reservations."

He was relaxing on the patio with Maddie and Tommy. Maddie's parents were inside, making some telephone calls.

"How did you talk them out of coming?" asked Maddie.

"I had to promise never to be alone for the rest of my stay here." Clive grinned. "Parents! I'm still not sure they won't pop over just the same."

"About that other kid on the plane," said Maddie, bursting with curiosity. "How do you suppose he got that package? Why didn't he give it to those guys himself?"

Mrs. Stoner had made an ice pack for Clive. He was holding it on his bruised lip. "I don't know."

"Maybe the package was hot," said Tommy.

"Hot?" Maddie looked puzzled.

"'Hot' as in stolen," said Tommy. "I can't believe you've never heard the expression." He sighed elaborately and started to say something sarcastic.

Maddie was about to jump up and bop him when Lieutenant Carlin appeared.

"Did you get them?" Clive asked eagerly. "Did you find those blokes?"

The detective shook his head. "The factory was empty when we got there. My guess is that they were already far away. But we found the room where you were held, Clive, and some evidence that may help us find them. First, I want to hear the whole story."

Lieutenant Carlin took out his notebook. With his questions, he led them through all the events of the day. But nobody said a word about the witch of Lancaster. They knew the police wouldn't believe anything they said if they brought up a ghost.

Then Clive told the detective about the other teenager on the airplane, and how he might be the one the men were after. "His name is Alan Devens," said Clive. "He lives in New York City, Lieutenant. He mentioned a place called Soho. I remember that because I've been to London. There's a Soho there, too."

Lieutenant Carlin wrote rapidly in his notebook. Then he snapped it shut and slipped it back into his pocket. "Don't worry," he assured them. "We'll look up this Alan Devens, and we'll get those two guys, too."

After the detective left, Clive asked, "So what about the witch?"

"What do you mean?" asked Maddie.

"You said she helped you find me."

Maddie told him how the ghost had led her and Tommy to the window of the abandoned factory.

"And she helped us find the button factory too," Clive recalled. He picked at his fingernail. "I don't understand. Why would she help me? I thought she hated me. I was sure she wanted to hurt me—even kill me. After all, she did push me at the pool, and later down the stairs."

"Maybe she just wants to scare you," said Maddie. "Maybe she wants something from you."

"What?"

"I don't know," Maddie admitted. She was as mystified as Clive. But one thing she knew for sure now: the witch of Lancaster existed. Even Tommy had seen it. And Tommy was the most practical kid on earth. He had no imagination at all. If he saw the witch, then it was really there.

Clive was being haunted by an ancient witch.

What did she want?

Ten

THE whole day had been a crazy jumble. First, the search for Clive, and the close call at the old factory. Then, dealing with their parents and the police. The questions and explanations seemed to go on forever.

And somewhere beyond the shadows hung the awful specter of the witch.

The Stoners ordered pizza for dinner and invited Tommy to stay, but he thought he'd better be going. His parents would be wondering by now.

Over pepperoni and cheese, the talk centered on Clive's kidnapping and rescue. Each time they heard additional details, Mr. and Mrs. Stoner became more agitated.

"Don't you *ever* even think of taking such

a chance again!" Maddie's mom ordered.

Maddie bit into her pizza without replying. Her thoughts kept shifting to the ghost.

After dinner, Clive asked Maddie if she wanted to go for a walk. Mrs. Stoner immediately objected. "No, Clive! It might not be safe."

"Please, Mrs. Stoner. I'd really like to go out," Clive said. "A walk would clear my head."

"Maybe Mom's right, Clive." Maddie felt a sudden tingle of fear. "Aren't you still scared?"

He nodded. "Sure, but I don't want to stay indoors the rest of my life."

Maddie's parents pointed out the dangers. But Clive was determined. Finally, Mr. Stoner gave in. "I guess it's okay. It's early. There are plenty of people out at this time."

"Don't go far!" Mrs. Stoner warned. "And be back in half an hour at the most."

Clive and Maddie slipped into the warm evening air before her parents could change their minds. The setting sun cast a gentle glow on everything as they walked slowly down the quiet street.

"I can't stop thinking about the witch," Maddie said.

"Me neither," Clive admitted.

"I wonder. . ." Maddie stopped suddenly.

"What?"

"How come Tommy and I were able to see her, but none of your friends and family in Morecambe did?"

"I've been thinking about that, too. . ." Clive paused. "But I think I've figured it out. I think she's getting stronger. When I first started seeing her a year ago, she wasn't clear at all. She was . . . sort of transparent."

"Well, she's definitely clear now!" Maddie said, calling to mind the face in the mirror.

"Right! And she's showing up more often, too. Somehow, she's getting stronger all the time."

For a few moments, they were each lost in their own thoughts. As they turned the corner, old Mr. and Mrs. Straus waved to them from their front porch. Maddie waved back. "I still can't figure her out though."

"Who?" Clive looked back at the house they had just passed. "That old lady on the porch?"

"No! The witch! It seems like she keeps trying to hurt you. And I was positive she was responsible when you were missing. But the opposite was true. She helped us find you." Maddie shook her head. "Why would she do that?"

"I don't know," Clive replied. "It doesn't make sense."

"Maybe she's trying to tell us something," Maddie mused.

"What?"

"You should know that better than me, Clive! You're the Bromley from Lancashire. You've read all those books." Maddie had a sudden thought. "What do the books say about ghosts?"

"Well, they say that ghosts are restless spirits. Instead of going to wherever it is that spirits go after death, they hang around here."

"Why?"

"Different reasons. Sometimes for revenge. Sometimes they're confused and don't know they're dead." Clive stopped abruptly. "Did you see that?" He pointed to a large black car that had passed them and was continuing down the block.

Maddie watched the car turn left a block away, then looked at Clive. He was pale. Maddie felt his fear jackknife into her.

Clive began to run in the direction the car had taken, pulling Maddie. "I think it's them—those two guys. Hurry!"

By the time they reached the corner, the car had disappeared. "Are you sure it was them?" Maddie asked. She looked around anxiously .

"I'm not positive," Clive replied. "But the car was black, and two men were inside."

"Did you see what they looked like?"

"No. I guess this whole thing has just freaked me out."

"Did you get the license number?" asked Maddie.

"No." Clive shook his head glumly. "I didn't think of it."

"Let's go home," Maddie suggested. The street ahead suddenly looked darker and more deserted.

"Maybe they're still after me. Or they think I'll lead them to Alan Devens."

"Nah!" Maddie tried to convince herself as well as Clive. "It probably wasn't them at all. You're just jumpy."

"I suppose you're right," said Clive. "I'll have to learn not to flip out every time I see a black car." He frowned. "But all the same, don't mention the car to anyone, Maddie. Your parents will tell mine and they'll make me come home right away."

Maddie agreed and they headed for home. "Clive, it's not a black car that's your problem," she said.

"You're talking about the witch, aren't you?"

"I'm thinking about what you said—about a ghost needing revenge. Maybe she wants something like that."

"The witch? That's impossible!" Clive protested. "I didn't hang her. I wasn't even around in the seventeenth century."

"Could it pass down through the family?" Maddie asked.

"Even if it did," Clive said, "what can I do about something that happened hundreds of years ago?" He sounded annoyed. They walked the rest of the way in silence.

There were two mysteries to be solved now. The kidnappers—had they really grabbed Clive by mistake? And, even more strange, the witch—why had she helped save

124

him from the kidnappers? Maddie's head ached from trying to figure it all out.

Clive must have been pondering the same things. "I *hate* that witch!" he said crossly. They had reached the Stoners' house and were cutting through the yard to go in the back way. "I wish she'd just go away and leave me alone."

Suddenly, a noise sounded from above. It began as a low groan, and quickly grew into a loud grinding crackle, as though the sky were splitting.

Maddie looked up and gasped. "Watch out, Clive!" she screamed. She shoved him so hard that he lost his balance and stumbled backward into a bush.

Less than a second later, a huge limb snapped off the tree. It crashed onto the spot where Clive had been standing, smacking the ground with a sickening thud.

Clive pulled himself up. "Maddie! If you hadn't pushed me out of the way, that would have fallen right on me! It could've killed me!" He bent down and examined the heavy limb with shaking hands. He looked at Maddie. "It was the witch, wasn't it? She did it."

"It was an accident, Clive," Maddie said. She decided not to mention that she was almost sure she had seen a face in the tree, just behind the curtain of leaves.

"I know it was her," Clive said bitterly. "It's so incredible! Earlier today, she helped save my life." He ran his hand down the length of the limb. "Now, she's trying to hurt me again. *Why?*"

Maddie had no answer.

Clive straightened up. "Let's look through my books. Maybe we can find a clue."

"Okay," said Maddie. By now, she didn't think there was any book that would solve their problems. But it was something to do.

When they went into the house, Mr. Stoner had news for them. "Lieutenant Carlin called. They checked out that boy in New York—that Alan something-or-other. He doesn't know anything about those men or about any package."

"Did the police believe him?"

"Yes, they found no reason to think he wasn't telling the truth."

Clive shrugged. "Maybe I was wrong about Alan." He started up the stairs. "Come on, Maddie."

They went into the guest room and began to flip through the books. Clive straddled Maddie's desk chair and picked up *Witches and Hauntings in England*. Maddie recognized it as one of the books he had checked out from the library.

"I haven't had a chance to look at this one yet," Clive said. He smoothed out a page. "Here's a section about the seventeenth century."

The words were hardly out of Clive's mouth when a noise like fingernails raking across a blackboard pierced the room. Maddie flinched and involuntarily glanced toward the window. Dread crept along her spine. "Look, Clive! There she is!"

Clive leaped to his feet and stared in horror. The head of the Lancaster Witch was suspended outside, glaring at them like a ghastly Halloween mask. Her pasty face glowed eerily in the dusk. Where her eyes should be were empty black circles.

Maddie shrank back. She opened her mouth to scream, but nothing would come out. She grabbed Clive's arm and dug her fingers into his flesh. He felt cold.

The terrifying skeletal hand of the witch

was scratching a message onto the glass.

"**P**..." the bony finger wrote. Then "**E**... **N**..." The letters seemed to be forming out of glistening particles of ice.

Maddie tightened her grasp on Clive. Her legs felt rubbery. Terror gripped the inside of her with the force of steel, squeezing her lungs until she could hardly breathe.

"**A**..." the dreadful finger drew in misty lines. "**N**..."

Shaking violently, Maddie was only dimly aware of Clive's own trembling reaction beside her. And still the scratching at the window went on, like claws dragged across a tombstone.

"**C**... **E**..." Maddie desperately wished she could look away. But her eyes had a will of their own. They stayed fixed on the window. Then, as abruptly as it began, the scratching stopped. No new letters appeared on the window.

"P," Maddie croaked, "E-N-A-N-C-E."

"*Penance*," Clive whispered.

Before they had a chance to think about the meaning of the ghostly message, the room exploded into horrifying chaos. The floor started to shake. Maddie and Clive struggled to keep their balance.

"Hold on!" Maddie yelled. Furniture shifted and slid across the floor. Objects began to fly about. Pens and paper clips zoomed through the air as if hurled by angry, unseen hands.

Maddie shrieked as a pencil sharpener hurtled past her and smashed against the wall. Books lifted themselves off the desk and traveled across the room. The desk chair skittered across the floor and banged into a wall.

"Stop!" Maddie screamed.

The commotion abruptly ended. The room and everything in it was still, as though nothing had ever happened. The message on the window had disappeared.

So had the ghost.

For a few moments, Clive and Maddie clung to each other. Then they began to pick things up and put them back into place.

"Where are your parents?" Clive asked. "They must be deaf not to have heard that racket." He looked down the hall. "I can't believe they're not running up here."

"That *is* weird," Maddie agreed. "They've probably got the stereo or TV turned up."

She placed the pencil sharpener back on the desk and gave Clive a frightened look. "Or maybe that show was meant just for us."

But Clive didn't seem to hear her. He was staring at a book that had been transported to a table across the room. "Maddie!" he whispered. "Come here!"

Maddie went over and looked at the book lying on the table. It was the one they had been looking at when the disturbance began. Now it was open to a page headed "The Lancashire Witches." One word, about half-way down the page, stood out from all the others. It shone with an eerie glow:

PENANCE

Maddie gasped. "It's the word that was on the window," she whispered. She lifted the book gingerly and read the text aloud.

"The spirit that has been torn from earthly life through injustice cannot rest until its death has been avenged. The murderer must be made to suffer. He must repent and perform penance before the unquiet spirit can find peace. If the murderer dies unrepentant, the haunting may continue for generations until a descendent of the original evil-doer enacts the penance. Only then can the unhappy spirit go to its rest."

Maddie stared at Clive. "Elizabeth Device wanted you to see this. She's telling you what to do."

"But why me?" Clive said. "And why after all this time? Why couldn't one of my ancestors have done this . . . penance?"

Maddie shrugged. "Maybe she tried earlier descendents. Maybe no one ever listened before." She pointed to Clive's books on witchcraft. "You showed her that you're interested."

They read on. For an unjust death by execution, two kinds of penance were described. The first involved suffering and dying in horrible pain by the executioner or his descendent.

"No way!" Clive exclaimed. "That's definitely out!"

Maddie agreed. "Here's the second way." She read aloud: "The murderer or his descendent may choose to perform penance by risking his life to save another person."

Clive brightened. "I could do that."

Maddie frowned. "Maybe you already did. Think. Have you ever saved someone's life?"

"I wish!" Clive replied. "But no."

"Maybe in the water. How about Morecambe Bay where you live? You're a good swimmer. Try to remember."

Clive grinned ruefully. "The only person who saved a life is you, Maddie. Twice. First, when you got me out of that factory, and then when you pushed me out of the way of that falling branch."

Maddie shook her head. "I don't think it counts if I do it."

Clive picked at a fingernail, already gnawed to the quick. "I guess not." He pointed to the book. "Does it say anything else?"

Maddie looked. The glow around the word "penance" had vanished. She examined the page headed "The Lancashire Witches," and those that followed. Then she put down the book. "That's it," she told Clive. "There's nothing else about penance. If you want to get rid of the witch, you have to die. Or save a life."

"Maddie?" There was a strange glint in Clive's eyes.

"What?"

"Let's go to the pool tomorrow. You could drown and I'll save you."

"That won't work, Clive!" Maddie shook her head. "*She'd* know it was phony. *She* probably hears every word we say." She met Clive's eyes. "Besides, I might really drown."

He grinned weakly. "I was only kidding, Maddie. Really."

Maddie felt ashamed. She should have known it was a joke. She was losing her sense of humor. Thanks to that awful ghost, she was forgetting how to have fun. She kicked at a pen that was still on the rug. "I *hate* the Lancaster Witch."

"Shh!" Clive put his finger to his lips. "She might be listening."

Was he joking? Maddie couldn't tell anymore. Everything had become serious—deadly serious. And it was all the fault of Elizabeth Device.

They had to find a way to get rid of her.

Eleven

MADDIE awoke with a start, as though someone, or *something*, had touched her. But there was nothing around, and she took a deep breath and willed herself to relax.

A few minutes later, she sat up and ran her fingers through her hair. Who was she kidding? Relaxation was impossible. Each day seemed to bring some new horror—ghosts, kidnappings, criminals. This was one year she wouldn't have to say, "Oh, the same old things," when asked what she did over the summer! But then again, what would she say?

Maddie got dressed and went down to breakfast. Her parents had gone to work early that morning to make up the time lost the day before. Maddie and Clive sat down at the kitchen table to talk about the witch's mysterious message: *penance*.

"We can get rid of the witch," Maddie said, "if we can figure out exactly what it means, and what it is Elizabeth Device expects you to do."

At a quarter to eleven, the doorbell rang.

"It's probably Tommy," said Maddie. She dashed to the front door.

But it wasn't Tommy at all. Standing outside was a lanky, sandy-haired teenager in tight jeans and a striped shirt with a designer label. He was carrying a knapsack.

"Hi," he said. "Is Clive here?"

"Clive?" Maddie was surprised. Other than those she had introduced him to, Clive didn't know anyone in the United States.

"I'm Alan Devens," the stranger said.

The boy who had been on the plane with Clive! The moment he said his name, Maddie noticed his resemblance to her cousin. Alan Devens was taller and thinner than Clive. His features were sharper, and his eyes a darker blue, but he looked enough like Clive to be mistaken for him.

Maddie's first thought was, *uh-oh, more trouble!* She felt a strong urge to slam the door in Alan Devens's face.

But Clive came up behind her. "Alan! How did you find me?"

"The cops told me where you were staying," Alan explained. "I took a bus out here." He reached into the knapsack and took out a package. "Guess what this is?"

Clive gasped. Maddie quickly pulled Alan Devens into the hall and shut the door. She and Clive stared at the package.

"Is that what those guys are after?" Clive asked.

Alan nodded.

"You lied to the police!" Maddie said. "You told them you didn't know anything about it!"

Alan ignored Maddie's accusation. He handed the package to Clive. "Look, Clive. I'm sorry about what happened to you. It was all a stupid mistake."

"That's easy for *you* to say!" Maddie's voice cracked. "Clive was hurt, and it could have been even worse!" Unable to conceal her dislike for Alan Devens, she snatched the package from Clive and examined it. It was about the size of an ordinary notebook, wrapped with heavy brown paper and sealed with gummed tape. It felt crinkly, as though a bunch of papers were inside.

"What's in it?" Maddie demanded.

Alan grabbed the package back out of her hands. "It's supposed to be art work, but I don't really know."

Maddie didn't like the way he had pulled it away from her. "Didn't you open it?" She raised her eyebrows and waited for an answer.

Alan shook his head. "Are you kidding? I'm in deep trouble with these guys already. They'd kill me if they thought I opened it."

Maddie shuddered. She had been right: Alan Devens was bringing big trouble. She wanted to shove him and his package right out of the house, but Clive said, "Let's talk about this."

He led Alan out the back door to the patio, and Maddie followed reluctantly. They already had more problems than they could handle, between criminals and a ghost. They didn't need Alan Devens and his package, too.

They all sat down, and Alan placed the

package on the table. It seemed to Maddie like a time bomb that could go off any minute.

"So, what's this all about?" Clive asked.

"It started at the airport in London. Do you remember, Clive, I told you I had been there with my Dad?"

Clive nodded. "You said he was staying another week in London. That's why you were traveling alone."

"Right." Alan acted as though Maddie weren't there. She was annoyed, but listened to every word. "I was waiting to board," Alan said. "Dad had gone to the men's room and I was sitting by myself. This guy came over and asked if I would like to make some easy money. I said 'sure.' He handed me the package and a fifty-dollar bill."

Clive's eyes never left Alan's face.

"I asked him what it was," Alan continued. "He said it was art he had bought in London—some famous sketches that weren't supposed to be taken out of the country. He said that there wouldn't be a problem if I stowed it in my backpack. Then I would just turn it over to some guys when I got to Kennedy."

"Guys?" Clive sat up straight. "What guys?"

Alan shrugged. "Just two guys. He was going to phone and tell them what I looked like. He said they'd find me."

Clive groaned. "They found me instead."

"I guess so," Alan said. "I waited, but no one ever came."

"So you kept the package?"

"I hid it in my closet at home. What else could I do?"

They sat quietly for a few moments. A red bird perched on the edge of the patio and chirped into the silence.

Maddie spoke first. "Why did you lie to the police?"

Alan turned to her as though he had just noticed she was there. "They told me what had happened to Clive. I was scared."

"Why are you here now?"

"To get rid of that!" Alan thumped the package with a finger. "I want to give it to those guys before they find out where I live and come after me."

Clive pointed out that no one knew where the men were.

"Yes, but they know where you are,

Clive," Alan replied.

Maddie remembered the black car Clive had seen the day before. She jumped up. "We've got to call my parents. And Lieutenant Carlin."

"Whoa!" Alan looked alarmed. "No way! This whole deal was probably illegal. I don't want any trouble with the cops. I already told them I don't know anything." His eyes narrowed. "If you tell anyone, I'll say you're lying. This has to be just between us." He looked from Maddie to Clive. "And anyway, I've got a plan."

Maddie started to object, but Alan cut her off.

"Here's what I've come up with," said Alan. "These guys already know you, Clive. I'm sure they're still watching you. All you have to do is take the package and walk around the neighborhood."

Clive opened his mouth to protest, but Alan held up his hand. "Let me finish. What you do is hold this package out so those guys can see it. When they do, they'll just grab the thing and that'll be the end of it." Alan smiled confidently. "It's simple."

"Simple for you," Clive grumbled. "What if

they grab me along with the package? They might decide they can't take a chance by having me as a witness."

Alan shifted uneasily. "There are some risks," he admitted. "But let's face it. Those guys won't give up until they get the package. And you're their only lead."

"I don't know," said Clive. He got up and paced around the patio. Then he came back and slammed his hand down on the table. "Why should *I* take such a risk?" he demanded.

"Because you're the one they're watching," Alan said.

Clive turned to Maddie. "What do you think, Maddie?"

Maddie put her hand on her cousin's arm. "Don't do it."

"Do you have any better ideas?" Alan challenged.

Maddie stood up, her hands on her hips. "Yes! Why don't you do it yourself, Mr. Alan Bigshot Devens? You're the one who got himself into this mess. You're the one who's afraid they'll come after you. *You* take the package."

"Me?" Alan looked bewildered. "But what

141

would be the point? It's Clive they know."

"They mistook him for you at the airport. Maybe this time they'll think that you're Clive. Besides," Maddie added triumphantly, "they'll recognize the package."

Alan rubbed his chin. "Uh . . . do you think it'll work?"

Maddie shoved the package at him. "Try it and see."

"Right now?"

"Sure!" Maddie stood. She pointed out the path that led around the house to the street. "We'll wait here."

Alan seemed confused. He stumbled as he stepped off the patio. "I . . . I'll walk around for half an hour," he said slowly. "If nothing happens, then I'll come back and, um, try again in a few hours."

Maddie nodded. "It might take a while. They're probably not watching all the time."

Alan's self-assurance had vanished altogether. He looked at Maddie with a lost expression. "You're right," he admitted. "I'm the one who screwed things up. I guess I got greedy. I'll do it myself." His shoulders slumped as he went down the path to the street. Soon he disappeared from view.

Clive looked troubled. "Maddie, this isn't right. He might get hurt."

"Clive, I can't believe you!" Maddie reminded her cousin what he had gone through when he was kidnapped and tied up in the old factory. "It was all because of Alan Devens," she said. "And now he asks you to do something risky."

"You're right," Clive agreed. "Even so . . ." He shook his head. "I don't know . . . it just seems wrong to let him go off alone." He stared at the spot where Alan had walked out of sight. "I'm going after him."

Maddie grabbed his arm. "Clive, please don't!" she begged. "Aren't you afraid of what those guys might do if they get their hands on you again?"

Clive pulled away. "Of course I am! I'm terrified! But even with what Alan did, I can't just turn my back on him."

Maddie followed anxiously as Clive began to walk down the path, but he told her to wait at the house. "If we're not back in half an hour," he said, "phone Lieutenant Carlin."

Now it was Clive who headed down the street. Maddie craned her neck to watch until she could no longer see him. As soon as he was gone, she was gripped by a premonition of disaster. This was too much like the time when Clive rode his bike out of Tommy's sight and disappeared. Despite the hot sun, Maddie shivered.

She forced herself to wait ten minutes. Never before had she felt so alone and helpless. If only her parents weren't at work!

She stared out at the street until her eyes ached. Finally, she could stand it no longer. She got up and rushed down the street where both boys had disappeared.

Twelve

TWO blocks from her house, Maddie came to the neighborhood park. It had a small playground in front and a large wooded area beyond. There were no children on the swings or slides. An elderly couple sat on a bench reading newspapers. Maddie recognized her neighbors, the Strauses.

It looked like just another ordinary day. But Maddie knew it wasn't. When she spotted a large black car parked on the street, her heart leaped into her throat. She got as close to the car as she dared, and risked a look inside. No one was there. But there were faint noises coming from the park—from deep in the wooded section.

Maddie ran down a narrow path that led

through the trees and bushes. As the sounds got louder, she could hear angry shouts. When she paused to get her bearings, she could feel her heart pounding in her chest.

Just as she prepared to sprint forward again, something caught her eye and caused her to look up. The sun was filtering through the tree leaves and reflecting an image through the branches. It looked like a long, white face. Maddie squinted to see better, and the image faded. Before she could give it another thought, she heard a thud and a wail. Maddie's mouth was dry with fear. She made herself race on.

In a few more seconds she came to a small, paved clearing, flanked by yellow benches. In the middle of the clearing were four figures. Two of them were tough-looking men. One was hefty and balding. The other was sharp-featured and dark.

Maddie recognized them instantly as the men she had seen at the factory. Both were bending over Alan Devens, punching him with their fists. He was crumpled up on his knees. His hands were covering his face, trying to protect it.

Maddie gasped, and her hand flew to cover her mouth.

Clive was standing behind the smaller man. He was tugging and pulling, trying to drag him off Alan. The man kept shoving Clive aside, and Clive kept coming back. Both men were shouting and cursing.

Maddie looked past the struggle to the edge of the clearing. Something caught her attention behind one of the benches. It was the Lancaster Witch! Her cape swirled about her skeletal figure. Against the pasty white of her face, her black eyes seemed to burn hotter than ever.

The witch's gaze was fastened upon Clive. She watched him with a strange intensity.

Numb with terror, Maddie tore her eyes away from the ghost. The big man had lifted his foot and given Alan a sharp kick in the side. Alan groaned, and the man reached into his pocket and brought out something that glinted. Maddie gasped. A *knife!*

Clive saw the knife, too. He seized the big man's arm, trying to grab the weapon. Cursing, the man turned on Clive and viciously shook him off. Then he pointed the knife straight at Clive. "You're asking for it,

x

x

x

kid!" he growled. The blade gleamed in the sun.

At that moment, Maddie heard someone screaming. Over and over again. Screams loud enough to wake the dead.

His arm in mid-air, the big man turned away from Clive, the gleaming knife still clutched in his hand. The other man stopped punching Alan and looked up. They stared furiously at Maddie. That was when she realized the screams were coming from *her*!

Suddenly, there were other noises and other voices. People were coming. Maddie heard footsteps rushing along the path.

"Let's get out of here," the big man muttered. Maddie spotted the package under his arm. He gave Alan one more violent kick, and both men ran off into the bushes.

Maddie turned her attention to the witch again. Something strange was happening— the witch's eyes were glowing like a candle-lit pumpkin. She was swaying from side to side. Her black-clad arms came out from under the cape, and she raised them high, as though in some sort of ghostly blessing. There was a low hissing sound, like air escaping from a balloon. Then, still swaying, the ghost began to fade. The eerie image grew dimmer and dimmer, until finally, it disappeared completely.

At that moment, several people burst into the clearing—a woman in jogging clothes and the Strauses. They helped Alan up.

"Are you all right?" Mrs. Straus said.

Alan nodded. His nose was bleeding, and he wiped it with his hand. "I'm okay. Just a little sore."

"I'd better go find a phone and call the police," said the jogger.

Alan shook his head. "No. That isn't necessary. It... it was just a misunderstanding." He stumbled toward Clive. "You saved my life, man. Thanks."

Saved my life. The words seemed important, but Maddie was too dazed to remember why.

"Let's go," said Clive. He started to lead Alan away. The three people came after them.

"Let me at least take you to the emergency room," the jogger said. "My car's parked nearby."

Alan shook his head. "Thanks a lot—

but really, I'm okay."

The adults looked doubtful as Clive tried to reassure them. "Maddie lives only a few blocks away. We'll call a doctor from her house."

Clive helped Alan down the path and out of the park. Maddie followed. She couldn't believe she had screamed so hysterically, but the scratchy soreness in her throat assured her that she had.

"I hope they don't call the police," Alan said. He was walking more easily with each step. By the time they got back to Maddie's house, he wasn't even limping. He looked at Clive and Maddie and grinned a crooked grin. "Well, we did it," he said. "We got rid of the package." He touched his face gingerly. His nose was no longer bleeding, but blood was still smeared over his bruised cheeks.

"Maybe you *should* see a doctor," Maddie said.

"No, I'll be okay." Alan clapped his hand on Clive's shoulder. "Thanks to Clive."

Clive shrugged. "You're the one who did it. You thought up the plan and you went out with the package."

Alan frowned. "I can't believe how mad

those creeps were! They said they'd teach me a lesson for holding out on them. They meant to slice me up. Did you see that knife?" He shuddered. "I hate to think what might have happened if Clive hadn't jumped that big guy."

Maddie wet a clean washcloth and handed it to Alan. He thanked her and wiped the blood from his face. "You saved my life, Clive," he repeated.

Saved my life. This time, Maddie understood.

"Clive!" she exclaimed. "You did it! You saved a life!" Now Maddie realized why the ghost of Elizabeth Device was in the park. She was watching Clive carry out the penance that would set her free.

Clive's face lit up. "The witch!" He exclaimed. "You know, I wasn't even thinking of her when I went after Alan."

"She was there," Maddie said. "Didn't you see her?"

Clive shook his head. "I guess I was too busy."

"She watched what you were doing. Then, she sort of faded away."

"Faded away?"

Maddie nodded. "She seemed different than before. When she disappeared, there was something sort of final about it. Like she was going away forever. She had her arms out like this." Maddie demonstrated. "As if she was saying goodbye."

Alan's expression showed confusion. "What are you talking about?"

Maddie and Clive exchanged glances. Clive nodded. "Let's tell him. After all, it's Alan who got me to pay the penance." He grinned. "Even though he didn't know he was doing it."

"Penance!" Alan broke in. "This is weird."

"Wait a minute." Maddie looked around curiously. "You know, something really *is* different. I can't exactly describe it. It's just something I feel."

"Me too!" Clive nodded. "It's like a clearness in the air." He gazed in all directions. "I always used to feel there was danger nearby. Like if I turned around, I'd see something. That feeling's gone."

"Will someone tell me what's going on?" Alan pleaded.

Maddie was almost starting to like Alan. He seemed more relaxed, nicer. Maybe it was because he had gotten rid of that package. The swagger he had put on when he first arrived was probably just an act to hide how scared he was.

"Let's tell him," Maddie said.

They took Alan upstairs and showed him the space on Maddie's wall where the mirror had hung. They described what had happened to the mirror, and the face that Maddie had seen in her window. Then they went into the guest room and told Alan about the commotion there. They related the whole story of the witches of Lancaster.

There was no expression on Alan's face. It was impossible to know what he was thinking.

"Do you believe us?" Maddie finally asked.

Alan looked around—at the books, at the window where the mysterious writing had taken place. He sighed. "No one could make up a story like that. It must be true." He turned to Clive. "Do you really think the ghost is gone now?"

Clive nodded.

The phone rang and Maddie picked it up. It was Mr. Straus.

"I thought you'd want to know," he said, "that we called the police right after you left. They just came by to tell us that they picked up those two men who attacked your friends."

"So fast?" Maddie couldn't believe it.

"They said a Lieutenant Carlin would be coming to see you. I got the impression he wants to thank you kids for being good citizens. Those men were caught with stolen goods."

"Stolen goods?"

"Some sort of artwork."

So Alan was right, Maddie thought. She thanked Mr. Straus for calling.

When she hung up, Clive called her over. "You want to hear something really strange, Maddie?"

Maddie couldn't imagine anything stranger than everything that had already happened. Then Alan repeated what he had told Clive.

"My family came here from England a long time ago," he said. "My great, great, great grandfather and his family." He paused, then went on. "They came from Lancaster."

"Lancaster?" That *was* weird.

"There's more," Clive said. "Tell her, Alan."

Alan looked at Maddie, mostly out of one eye. The injured one was almost closed now. "It's about our family name."

"Devens?"

"Right. It's changed over the years. Other branches of the family have different names. My grandfather talks about it a lot. I've heard him mention names like Devers, DeVons, and..."

"And what?" Maddie asked impatiently. She realized she was holding her breath.

"I think he said Device, too."

Was it possible? Could Alan Devens be a descendent of Elizabeth Device? Had Clive saved the life of someone actually related to the witch?

"Did anyone in your family ever mention the Lancaster witches?" Maddie asked.

Alan shook his head. "No. I never heard of them. There's probably no connection."

Maybe not, Maddie thought. And yet...it would be just one more reason for Elizabeth Device's ghost to be able to go to her rest. Maddie seized her cousin's hand. "She's gone, Clive! I know it!"

A broad smile spread across Clive's face. "I feel the same way, Maddie. I'm really free now. I can tell."

Maddie nodded. What a relief! Now she could get on with her real life, with her normal summer activities.

She looked out the window. The sun was shining and it was still early. "Hey, guys," she said, "let's go to the pool."

There will be no tall, dark figure behind the bushes to scare us this time, Maddie thought happily. And, oh, what a story she'd have for Chloe when she finally came home from vacation!

Afterword

The basic story of the witches of Lancashire is true to history. Ten women were accused of witchcraft in 1612 and hanged in front of Lancaster castle. One of them was Elizabeth Device. The judge who ordered their execution was named Lord Bromley.

All other characters and events in this story come only from my imagination.

—*Carol H. Behrman*

About the Author

Carol H. Behrman was born in Brooklyn, New York, and now lives in Fair Lawn, New Jersey, with her husband, Edward.

Besides teaching writing workshops and speaking at writers' conferences, she has written more than ten novels for children and young adults. She is also the author of several nonfiction books and a writing text for students in grades five through eight.

She got many of her ideas for her novels from the experiences of her children as they were growing up. Other ideas were inspired by students at the middle school in Glen Ridge, New Jersey, where the author taught for many years.

Besides writing, Carol H. Behrman enjoys traveling, crossword puzzles, and reading.

The Lancaster Witch is her first book for Willowisp Press.